THE PENNYFIELDS

OTHER TITLES BY DIANA PULLEIN-THOMPSON IN THE
ARMADA SERIES INCLUDE

HORSES AT HOME

THREE PONIES AND SHANNAN

RIDING WITH THE LYNTONS

JANET MUST RIDE

© DIANA PULLEIN-THOMPSON 1949

The Pennyfields was first published in the U.K. in 1949 by Wm Collins Sons & Co. Ltd, London and Glasgow. This edition was first published in 1964 by May Fair Books Ltd, 14 St. James's Place, London, S.W.1, and was printed in Great Britain by Love & Malcomson Ltd, Brighton Road, Redhill, Surrey.

DIANA PULLEIN-THOMPSON

The Pennyfields

COVER ILLUSTRATION
BY PETER ARCHER;

TEXT ILLUSTRATIONS
BY DYLAN ROBERTS

ARMADA
PAPERBACKS
for Boys & Girls

"I only want enough money to pay my fare home"

Chapter One

DOWN in the valley, between Trushfield and Scholar's Water, there dreams a house, which is white where the dark holly, the jasmine and the roses do not clamber, which is green-windowed and older even than the great oak that stands—a tall sentinel—by the garden gate. Only a rough lane leads to it, winding beneath countless elms, which are rugged and dangerous when the wind is strong, but true friends on a hot August day.

Here, in summer, cows wander, stopping occasionally to pick juicy mouthfuls of the fragrant meadowsweet on their way to the ramshackle byre, that stands in the small square yard close to the house. Here, too, the Pennyfield children may be seen—tall, dark Lucien, good-looking Marie, paler, quieter Sheila, serious Paul, bouncing, bespectacled Jennet and the two youngest—cheerful, slap-dash Charles and tireless Lottie.

An odd assortment of animals may be with them: Janet and Judas, the ferrets, or Tick and Tock, the mice, might be in the boys' pockets; somebody will be riding the little grey donkey, Dandylion. Two or three dogs are sure to be there and perhaps a tortoise; and, in all probability, the quiet meadows, the wooded hills will ring with the sound of Pennyfield voices; for the Pennyfields are a noisy family.

On the sunlit spring day when this story starts, they were sitting astride a fallen apple tree holding a council of war. Lucien was speaking; Marie, solemn, brown-eyed and dark-haired, was listening; Sheila was gazing into the distance, across a rolling green meadow into the cool beechwoods; Paul, most like Marie, was also intent with his rather pronounced chin resting on his hand; fair-headed Jennet was bouncing up and down, longing to interrupt her eldest brother; Charles, untidy in ragged shorts, was peel-

5

ing bark off the tree trunk; Lottie, his twin, stood, a gap of bare back showing between her pullover and shorts, patting Dandylion's hard grey neck.

"For too long we have been poverty stricken," said Lucien. "For too long we have awaited miracles—for Daddy to win the Irish Sweepstake, for Marie to write a best seller, for some wretched rich relative to die. It is time for action. I am tired of being poor—we all are. Well, let's mend matters. Don't let's sit back and go without things any more. Let's work and work, really get to and make some money, start a new campaign. We could run a carrier service with Dandylion, catch a mass of rabbits with Janet and Judas, dig our small patches of garden and sell vegetables; but make some money we must. Do you all agree?"

"Yes," answered every one.

"We might start a magazine," suggested Marie.

"I could borrow Daddy's typewriter and take in some typing," added Sheila in her quiet voice; she was the least noisy of the Pennyfields.

"What about a circus?" shrieked Lottie.

"We could act a play," said Jennet.

"Let's start a list of ways and means of earning money," suggested Paul.

"Head it with ferreting," Charles spoke.

"No, *circus*. Dandylion can stand on a tub and Brockie jump through a hoop," cried Lottie.

"Do be quiet a moment, please," said Paul. "Let's see— Typing, Gardening, Ferreting."

"Circusing," interrupted Lottie.

"All right, in a minute," Paul told her. "Acting, Circusing, Something with Dandylion—any more suggestions?"

"Let's make a list of what we are going to buy with the money we earn, that's much more exciting," suggested Jennet.

"A pony," shrieked Lottie.

"A canoe," shrieked Charles.

"For me, a horse or, if the money doesn't go as far, a double-barrelled shotgun—that'll help make more," said Lucien.

"We'll all have lots of nice things," said Jennet gaily.

"Can't we make a list when the time comes for spend-

6

ing?" said Marie, passing a hand across her exceptionally high forehead.

"We could raffle something," said Lottie.

"Not in aid of ourselves," Sheila told her.

"Why not?"

"Oh, don't be silly," said Jennet.

"It would be wrong—false pretences," said Sheila.

"Nonsense," said Lottie. "We could tell them it was in aid of ourselves; no one would mind."

"What, go round begging?" asked Paul. "Have you no scruples?"

"It wouldn't be begging; it would be a raffle. Anyway, I don't know what scruples mean."

"Do stop arguing. I'm sure it would be illegal. I think you are forced by law to give the proceeds to some registered charity," said Lucien, and finished the matter.

"We've got enough ways to go on with," said Paul, twiddling his chewed red pencil. "Let's get to work immediately."

"You've forgotten Magazine," Marie reminded him.

"We must get the campaign a bit organised—fix up dates for play and circuses and everything—christen the magazine—decide what each of us will grow in our garden," said Lucien.

"I vote we have the circus these holidays," cried Lottie.

"I don't agree; if we leave it to the summer, everybody will be better trained," contradicted Marie.

"Well, what are we going to do *these* holidays?" asked Charles, plunging his hands into the pockets of his grey flannel shorts.

"Start the magazine, sow things in our garden, find some jobs for Dandylion and start training for the circus," answered Marie.

"We could have a variety show," said Jennet. "Sheila could sing, Paul recite . . ."

"And Lucien make puppets," added Sheila, staring at the clear sky with pale blue eyes.

"I'll tell you what we could do—serve teas under the chestnuts at the top of the lane," said Marie.

"Bags make the cakes," shouted Jennet.

"Oh, I wanted to!" wailed Lottie, vaulting on Dandylion.

"I think we ought to have a special target, aim at making a hundred pounds by next spring. We could make a chart, like they have for savings campaigns, and move the arrow, or whatever it is, up each week," said Lucien.

"We could paint a horse at the top, because that's what we all really want," added Lottie.

"I think it would be horrible; it reminds me of the war. Anyway, I hate charts and diagrams," said Marie.

"I know what I shall do tomorrow," declared Jennet. "I shall take Dandylion up to the bus stop, when the twelve-ten arrives, and relieve every one, who has to walk far, of their shopping bags and deliver them at their homes for a few pence."

"Oh *I* wanted Dandylion to practise for the circus," shrieked Lottie.

"You might as well deliver the people themselves, while you're about it," observed Paul.

"Let's board dogs," said Lottie, owner of a grasshopper mind.

"I don't think Daddy would like it," Sheila told her.

"Let's stop making mad suggestions and try to get a few things straight," said Lucien.

"Boarding dogs wasn't a mad suggestion," interrupted Lottie indignantly.

"Is a hundred pounds to be our aim?" Lucien went on, deliberately ignoring his youngest sister.

"A pretty steep one," remarked Sheila.

"Too steep?" questioned Lucien.

"I think we might achieve it if we really worked and, after all, we can't get ponies, guns and canoes with much less." Marie unconsciously put them in the order that they ranked in her mind; ponies were, of course, to her the most important item.

"Gosh, think what we could buy!" exclaimed Jennet, and she pictured piles of crisp pound notes.

"Does every one agree on a hundred pounds to be earned by April the Fourth of next year?" asked Lucien.

"All right," said Marie, and she seemed to answer for the others, who merely nodded their approval.

8

"Right," continued Lucien, sounding brisk and businesslike. "Does every one agree to cultivate their gardens? Sheila will you pull up some of your flowers and plant vegetables instead?"

"I'll pull up the flowers, which I can't sell," consented Sheila.

"I'll try to garden, but it makes my arms ache," said Charles.

"Oh, don't be feeble," said Jennet, bouncing up and down on the tree trunk.

"I'll sow my garden and grow mustard and cress in boxes too, and help Charles when his arms ache," answered Lottie, who was really the kindest hearted of the Pennyfields.

"I would like to grow something special like asparagus," Marie said.

"I don't think vegetables like me, but I will have a shot," said Paul.

"I don't think asparagus will bring in any money for some time," said Lucien; "we are starting rather late in the year anyway. Most people sow in February. Still, there's an old gardening book in the toolshed; perhaps it can tell us something."

"Well, *that's* settled," said Marie firmly, "we are all going to garden. Now, let's decide who's going to be editor of this magazine."

"You, of course," said Paul, "you're the literary one."

"What nonsense; you write poetry and Lucien wrote a most erudite article on chimney-pieces the other day," said Marie.

"Well, you write the most and anyway it was your idea," said Paul.

"Of course you should be editor, Marie," said the twins and Jennet in chorus; and so Marie accepted the post. Then Jennet started talking about the variety show. "It would bring in an awful lot of money. Lucien and Sheila could make the puppets. Sheila could sing. Charles could play a tune on his mouth organ. The dogs could do a little act and we could have a tug-of-war or wrestling match and give an acrobatic display on Dandylion. I'm sure lots of people would come and we could charge sixpence a seat."

So it went on—the planning and the arguing, until old Mrs. Tibbles, who had come as nurse when Lucien was born and, since Mrs. Pennyfield died on a wet March day soon after the twins were born, had been almost in sole charge of the children during holiday time, went out into the orchard and told them that they must come in and lay the tea.

Even then, hurrying indoors, they thought about their new campaign. Lucien saw his goal, a bay hunter with black points standing in the old brick and flint stable by the house. Marie saw a neat fat magazine with a striking but tasteful cover, designed by Lucien. Sheila saw her father, tall, dark, serious, listening as they told him about the money they had made. We must spend some of it on a surprise for him, she thought. Paul saw scores of ducks quacking gaily, lying in the sunlit orchard amongst the yellow daffodils; for Paul had a passion for ducks, especially Aylesburys, which he thought exceptionally cheerful. Jennet saw the long, narrow lane, that leads to the bus stop; she saw Dandylion's back and the collar and a pair of large pricked ears; she felt each familiar bump, as she stood up in the yellow and red cart, and the skies were blue and the sun as hot as to-day. Charles saw a canoe with two seats, long and varnished, and felt his paddles dipping into the rippling water and his heart beating as he quested adventure in rivers unexplored. Lottie saw Dandylion on a scarlet tub and Brockie, who was a tireless little terrier and belonged to Sheila and Paul, jumping through a hoop, and a crowd cheering and clapping, as though their enthusiasm would never end.

In the long cool dining-room, the children laid tea, their sandshoes making little noise as they hurried to and fro on the uneven stone floor, fetching the chipped yellow plates, the mugs, with French peasants painted on them, which their father had brought them from Brittany, the rough new bread, the golden syrup, the much cherished honey, pale war-time butter, milk fresh from the farm and all the usual knives and spoons.

Outside, in the orchard, a golden sun peered through the

white cherry blossom and bade good night to the landscape, which, but an hour before, had been bright with spring colours, alive with birdsong. And Paul's two ducks wended their way homewards, through the grass to their yellow house; and the guinea fowl gazed up at the elder tree and thought of sleep; and the ferrets clawed at their wire netting and hoped that supper would not be long in coming; and the two white mice slept in their cage in the granary.

Chapter Two

IT WAS the day after the council of war and the sun was shining, as Lucien walked, hands deep in the pockets of his corduroy trousers, in the direction of Thrushfield Post Office. Soloman, the tall sable and white collie, followed at his heels. Lucien held three notices inside a pocket. They asked: *Are your windows dirty? Why not employ The Scholar Farm Quick Window Cleaning Service? This excellent body will clean all your windows, inside and out, at express speed, with a minimum amount of noise and bother for a 1/- per window. Tel. Thrushfield 100.* And: *The Scholar Farm Quick Washing Up Service will wash up in your house after parties, with speed and efficiency, at minimum cost. Ring Thrushfield 100.* And: *Anything moved anywhere within a 10-mile radius by The Scholar Farm Transport Department. Orders dealt with promptly and efficiently. Tel. Thrushfield 100.*

He was not in a very good temper; he had wakened early with a feeling that something exciting was about to happen and, in fact, the morning had turned out to be tedious and tiresome. His brothers and sisters had argued for hours over the three advertisements and then, at the finish, they had all voted against him when he objected to *this excellent body.* The money situation was disappointing; with great difficulty, they had persuaded Tibbles to surrender their Post Office savings books, which she always kept in a locked drawer, for a few hours; but only to find that, between all seven of them, they could not rake up more than twelve pounds, some of which would be needed for advertising, buying seeds for the garden, buying a new ribbon for the typewriter and paper and also for buying beehives, because Sheila had decided that she would like to keep bees and sell honey.

He felt that the circus would be a flop and the variety show a noisy muddle and he could not think of anything to write for the magazine. It was annoying, too, to be in a bad temper on a fine day; it seemed almost ungrateful, when the sun was making his back so pleasantly warm and the little whitewashed cottages and the toy-like fields in the valley and the cherry blossom and the blue sky were looking so beautiful, when all the land seemed to be rejoicing, because spring was here. What right had he to be cross?

It was in this unsatisfactory state of mind that Lucien entered the post office and produced his advertisements. The postmistress, a fat, flabby, bespectacled woman, who reminded him suddenly of liver sausages, was surprisingly agreeable. She made none of the disparaging comments which he had expected; in fact she barely read the advertisements, being in such haste to pin them in a prominent position. Then, to Lucien's amazement, the charge was only sixpence a week for the three; so he was able to put away the ten-shilling note, which he had expected to cash if not spend, and give her half a crown instead. This changed his mood at once and, being at heart an optimist, he immediately became certain that things were taking a turn for the better. After cheerfully admiring the postmistresses's old Scottie and remarking on the lovely weather, he left the shop and, whistling "The Blue Danube", started his homeward journey.

He was wondering whether Marie had been so successful on her identical errand to The Scholar's Water Post Office, when he became aware of excited voices. Looking over a sprawling thorn hedge on his left, he saw, at the bus stop ahead, Jennet, Dandylion and Brockie and a small crowd of villagers. He was filled with trepidation. His first thought was: an accident—Lottie or Charles—dead—broken-legged—squashed. For Lucien was always afraid that, one day, his youngest brother and sister would kill

12

themselves; they were so silly—always playing the fool and doing silly things.

At school they had learned the "daring habit" and now they were for ever daring each other to jump off roof tops, walk barefoot through nettles, wink at policemen and attempt many other futile and dangerous feats. Tibbles frequently told him that, being the eldest, he should control the twins and break them of their "foolish ways." She was also inclined to say that she was busy in the house and that he must be responsible for them for the day. He had a horrible feeling now, that to-day was one of those days. Had not she said something of that sort at breakfast? It would be awful enough if they had been run over, without him being to blame as well.

He broke into a jog trot and then, as he drew nearer, he noticed to his relief that there was no corpse lying in the road, nothing to suggest a bad or fatal accident and, best of all, no sign of the twins. An old woman was picking something up off the road. Jennet was talking very loudly and gesticulating like a foreigner. Dandylion was grazing, his little red and yellow cart perched precariously on the bank. Oh dear! thought Lucien, what can have happened? I hope Jennet hasn't knocked someone over. She's really got no consideration for the aged.

Suddenly, she saw him. "Lucien, Lucien, do come and help. I've bust a basketful of eggs and Mrs. Smiley wanted them for lunch."

Her voice was much too cheerful for one who has just foolishly destroyed a basketful of valuable rationed food.

"*Lunch* indeed! I like that!" exclaimed the woman, who had been picking something up off the road. "There were a good dozen there—'ave done for many a meal, they would—many a meal. Charging sixpence indeed for taking me 'ome and then going and breaking the w'ole blooming lot."

"Not quite," said Jennet. "There are these two, which fell on the bank. I'm most awfully sorry. I didn't mean to upset the cart, but you know what donkeys are."

"There's only one thing to do," said Lucien. "Either we replace the eggs when we can or pay you what they are worth."

"But look," cried Jennet. "There's no reason why we should pay damages. There's a notice in the cart, saying: *Parcels and humans travel at their own risk. Should an accident occur, there will be no commemoration.* It's as large as life and I know the spelling's right, because I looked the long words up in the dictionary."

Lucien is tiresome, she thought, always too willing to pay damages or replace things. She added a trifle proudly, because she felt that this notice of hers showed some foresight and a businesslike mind: "I thought something awful might happen (you know what Dandylion is) so I pasted it on as large as life."

Lucien was furious. It was just like Jennet to be so utterly tactless. Now nobody would want to employ *The Scholar Farm Quick Window Cleaning Service, The Scholar Farm Quick Washing-Up Service* or *The Scholar Farm Transport Department.*

"For goodness' sake be quiet," he whispered, and then to Mrs. Smiley, he said: "I'm very sorry that this has happened. The donkey normally behaves very well and I'm sure my sister would not have taken you and your eggs if she had any idea that she might misbehave to-day. Please may we have the pleasure of paying you the value of the eggs?"

"I don't want your money, young man—thanks all the same. Of course we all know that accidents must 'appen and it's no good crying over spilt milk. But I'm blessed if I'll take another ride in that blooming donkey cart."

"For the sake of our consciences then, please may we replace the eggs?" asked Lucien.

"Consciences indeed! I bet you two 'ave got a couple of fine consciences,' 'said Mrs. Smiley, and at this remark the few remaining villagers burst out laughing, as if consciences had never been heard of in the Pennyfield family.

Lucien grinned and then Mrs. Smiley went on: "Still, if you would like to replace the eggs, I won't say no—seeing that they're so 'ard to come by."

Jennets face fell. "Right you are," said Lucien. "If you can come down to the farm, I expect we could give you a few now. Or would you prefer us to deliver them at your house? I'm afraid I'm not sure where you live." He spoke

14

apologetically, because Mrs. Smiley's face was familiar and he was sure that he had seen her many, many times at a garden gate—a rather shabby green one—but where that gate was or to what cottage it belonged he had no idea.

"Why, down yonder, of course. I was there the other day when you passed with a ferret in your pocket—at the gate. 'Course you know it."

"Oh yes. How silly of me—of course, of course," said Lucien, and his sister thought he sounded like a doddering old man, and Mrs. Smiley laughed a little scornfully and said:

"Well, if you would be so kind as to deliver them, that would be very nice—more 'andy like, than me coming to your place."

"Mind, don't you try a-taking them in that there donkey cart though," advised a farm labourer.

"Right you are then, that's fixed; I expect we'll be up to-morrow and if we can make it a dozen eggs we will," said Lucien, and then he and his sister walked briskly after Dandylion, who, having become tired of waiting, was sauntering away down the road.

"What a stingy woman," said Jennet.

"What on earth happened?" asked Lucien.

"And you just played into her hands. Why did you have to offer her twelve eggs when I only broke ten? Anyway, we needn't have returned any, with that notice in the cart."

Lucien was used to Jennet's habit of evading answering one question by asking another, so he merely said: "You put commemoration instead of compensation. But, what did you do to upset the basket?"

"What did I do? You mean, what did *Dandylion* do?"

"I mean, what happened? Do come to the point," said Lucien, exasperated.

"She wanted to go home and Mrs. Smiley wanted to go up towards Thrushfield, and when I hit her she backed into the ditch and the eggs and Mrs. Smiley fell out. I *did* try to stop her and I *did* tell Mrs. Smiley that she was travelling at her own risk. After all, when the cleaners made a hole in my frock they didn't pay anything; they

15

said I had sent it at my own risk and pointed to a horrible little notice on the wall."

"We've got to think of our reputation," said Lucien. "It's not as though we've already done a lot of work for people with Dandylion. I mean we mustn't annoy our customers the very first time; if it was just one accident out of twenty journeys it would be different."

"It means we've just lost money this morning," remarked Jennet mournfully.

"That's your fault, not mine. You should improve your driving. Dandylion doesn't behave like that with Marie."

"Well, where are we going to get the eggs, which you so rashly promised?"

"Flippy and Flappy might have laid; we'll have to try and buy the rest, probably at black-market price. We could ask Mr. Bennet."

"Oh no! He's always so disagreeable."

"Only with you and the twins, because you will run across his fields. After all, you wouldn't like it if our orchard was always full of shouting, dirty children."

"I bet he charges a lot."

They had arrived at Scholars Farm now and Lottie came tearing down the garden path to tell them that it was long past lunch and that Tibbles was in an awful rage. Lottie always exaggerated Tibbles' anger, so Jennet did not worry much. Anyway, Lucien could easily talk round the nurse, who generally believed his excuses. He said now: "If you'll deal with Dandylion, Jennet, I'll go and calm Tibbles."

"It's all right," cried Lottie, "I've had lunch; I'll deal with her, but what on earth happened to you?"

The donkey, having arrived at her destination, had stopped and was peacefully eating grass at the entrance of the farmyard.

"I've made a hash of things and Lucien is going to spend masses of money putting it right," Jennet said.

"We must go in. Come on," urged Lucien. "Thank you, Lottie," he added.

"Wait for me before you tell the others what happened," she shouted, taking hold of the little grey donkey.

It *was* from Mr. Bennet that they eventually bought a dozen eggs. They paid three shillings for them, which was slightly less than his usual black-market price. Flippy and Flappy had laid, but Tibbles had taken their eggs for a pudding. Lucien said it was Jennet's job to walk up to Mrs. Smiley's cottage and Jennet said it wasn't—Lucien had offered to deliver the eggs, not her. Eventually Lucien fetched the rest of the family to help decide and they all agreed that, as he had already walked to Thrushfield Post Office, there was no doubt at all that it was Jennet's job to take the eggs.

The next difficulty was that no one seemed to know where Mrs. Smiley lived. Jennet had merely asked, "Right or left?" and the answer only proved that it was somewhere in the Thrushfield direction. Of course, Lucien knew that it had a green gate. But Jennet, who was rather obstinate over the whole affair, said she was sure she would never find it. Lottie offered to accompany her and then Charles screamed that she had promised to help him with his garden. Then Paul had a brainwave and suggested ringing up the Post Office and asking them where Mrs. Smiley lived. Lucien thought it a good idea and got through in a few minutes, only to find that it was more complicated than he had imagined it would be.

Apparently there were two Mrs. Smileys and both were fat and both about fifty-five; one, the postmistress said, was blue-eyed and the other brown-eyed, but they both had grey hair, although one arranged hers in a bun, while the other left hers plain bobbed. Lucien remembered that *their* Mrs. Smiley had been wearing a hat and the postmistress asked what kind of hat? and, of course, he could not remember at all, which she said was tiresome, because the Mrs. Smiley what lived down by the church always wore an old tammy with a hat pin, and so if he had only been a little more observant and noticed, she could have easily told him which one it was they wanted. He mentioned the green gate, but the postmistress said they both had green gates; you see they were sisters, who had married cousins and they both liked the same things. Then the postmistress remembered that one had a light green gate and the other a dark green gate. "Now, which did *your*

Mrs. Smiley have?" she asked, and Lucien had to admit that he didn't know, and she said what a pity; if only he had known she would have been able to tell him which Mrs. Smiley he wanted. Lucien was becoming tired of the conversation and, at every opportunity, he tried to end it.

"Never mind," he said, whenever he could get a word in, "we'll try both houses. Let's see, one's by the church."

But the postmistress seemed intrigued by the dilemma and would not stop talking; while, outside, Marie chanted *hurry up*, because Tibbles had asked her to ring up the grocer and she wanted to finish the story she was writing for the magazine and not spend all the remaining afternoon waiting for Lucien.

At last the postmistress said, "Well, I should try both cottages—might as well—that's what I should do. Now, Mrs. Bob Smiley, the one what wears the tammy, lives close to the church—number nine it is and the only one with a green gate and Mrs. *Jim* Smiley, the one what 'as the bun, she lives three houses beyond Bullett's, the bakers —an 'ouse with a gable and a bit of lace at the front window—you can't miss it—three houses beyond Bullet's . . ."

She repeated her directions three times before Lucien was able to thank her profusely and ring off.

"Never again will I ring up the Post Office for any information whatsoever," he vowed. "She thinks I'm mad anyway, because I couldn't remember what sort of hat the woman was wearing. You can't remember, I suppose, Jennet, can you?"

"Yes, of course I can—a brown mushroom sort of hat with a large pin. Is it the missing clue?"

"Yes, but, oh gosh! I can't remember now whether it was the tammy or the other hat, which lived by the church. Oh dear! It's enough to drive a person mad. I think I had better come with you, Jennet. Come on. It'll give the dogs another walk."

"While you've been telephoning, we've done all the washing up," said Lottie.

"How marvellous," said Lucien. "Dogs, dogs, dogs. Come along—walkies, walkies. Cockade, you lazy girl, where are you?"

The dogs arrived, one by one, the old White West Highland last. Then Jennet collected Chunky, her tortoise, who had wakened up before the other tortoises, and Lucien the basket of eggs and they set off.

It was a good mile to the first cottage and they were drenched by a shower on the way; but the first cottage was the right one and the Mrs. Smiley, with the bun and brown eyes, opened the door and Lucien knew at once that she was not the sort of woman to wear a tammy. She looked at the basket of lovely brown eggs and said that it was very nice of him to bring a dozen, and then she took them, a little too quickly to be described as politely. Her husband was eating his tea with his sleeves rolled up and a solemn expression on his rough obstinate face. And when Lucien saw Mr. Smiley, he could have kicked himself; for he had seen this man scores of times before and remembered now that he was Miss Summer's gardener. Miss Summers was a fussy little woman, who lived in a large dark house close to the Post Office and hated the Pennyfields' dogs, because she was afraid they might hurt Jock, her Skye terrier. And, of course, Lucien had known all the time that the gardener's name was Smiley and, if he had had any sense, would have connected things up and saved himself trouble.

The old couple were very agreeable and gave each of the three dogs a biscuit and asked, rather laughingly, whether Lucien was going to start cleaning windows now. He said yes. And Mr. Smiley said he had better be a-seeing Miss Summers then. For 'pon his word, you could hardly see out of some of her windows.

So the egg episode really ended quite agreeably and Lucien felt that, by replacing the loss, he had saved the Scholar Farm reputation; but both he and Jennet felt that the fact that they had lost three shillings on the very first day of their campaign was very disconcerting indeed.

"To-morrow," said Lucien, "we really must make some money. Perhaps someone will ring us up and ask us to wash up or move something. Mr. Smiley had obviously heard about the advertisement. The news will soon get around. I never asked Marie what Mr. Sims at Scholar's Water thought about it."

"I *do* want to school Dandylion a bit though," said Jennet.

Chapter Three

THE very next day, as a result of the Pennyfields' advertisements, the telephone rang not once, but three times. Lucien, who was making his bed, answered the first ring. It was a Mrs. Saunders wanted to know whether *The Scholar Farm Quick Window Cleaning Service* could clean all her windows inside and out, as soon as possible, because she was giving rather a large and important party in the evening. Lucien was pleased to say that they could do the job this morning. "We'll be along just before eleven," he told her. And she said: "That sounds too good to be true. I had given up all hope of getting them done until I saw your little notice in the Post Office yesterday. There are ten windows and I've got one ladder if you like to borrow it, but I expect you've got your own."

"Thank you very much," said Lucien, calculating swiftly and thinking: hurray, ten bob.

"Well, I'll be seeing you and your men at eleven then. Your firm's advertisements have bucked me up no end. I really feel we are beginning to get back to pre-war days at last."

Lucien knew he ought to have nipped the delusion in the bud and told Mrs. Saunders that his assistants were children, not men, but he funked it and merely said: "I'm so glad. Eleven then, Madam. Thank you," and rang off.

Then Lucien called his sisters and brothers, but on getting no reply, he decided that they must be outside and that he would tell them the good news when they came in. Whistling "The Chocolate Soldier," he wandered back to his bedroom, finished making his bed and then ran up to the attic to fetch a step-ladder.

Meanwhile Paul, who had been feeding his two ducks and trying to compose a sonnet worthy of them—a task he had been attempting for the last year—came indoors, heard the telephone and answered it. A thin fragile voice asked if *The Scholar Farm Transport Department* could take a trunk to the station and send it off on the eleven-ten Birmingham train.

Paul said: "Yes, certainly, Madame, with pleasure. Just tell me your address and we will be at your door in no time."

The fragile voice said: "How very kind. Now that is nice. My name's Parker—Miss Parker—and I live at Woodside, it's got a gable and an iron gate, a black one, and it's quite close to the Post Office. Do you know Miss Summers' house—well, it's next to that."

"Right," said Paul, feeling rather important and very businesslike, "We'll be round right away."

He put down the receiver with a cheerful smile. The others *will* be pleased, he thought, and then the telephone rang again. This time a man's voice inquired whether he was speaking to the manager of the *Scholar Farm Quick Window Cleaning Service*. Paul said no; he was speaking to one of the assistant managers, who would be very pleased to help him in any way. The man said that he did not wish to speak to any assistants; he wanted to speak to the manager and that his name was Major Davis.

Paul said, "Okay," and then, thinking that he had sounded a little casual, added, "Yes, sir, I will fetch him at once." He yelled to Lucien and Lucien, who was coming down the stairs with an extremely dusty step-ladder on his shoulders, said, "This is wonderful. Two people in the course of half an hour."

"You mean five minutes," corrected Paul, thinking that his brother was alluding to the fragile woman and her trunk.

Then Lucien spoke to Major Davies, who said that he wanted his motor mower transported from the Long White House to the Corner Garage as soon as possible. "I particularly wished to speak to you," he explained, "because I want you to ask your men to be very careful of my mower. Last time I got Badens to take it and they bent the box and damaged the carburettor."

"Right you are, sir. Every care will be taken," Lucien said, and wished again that he was brave enough to explain that there were no men in his firm, only children.

"What time can you come?" asked Major Davis.

21

"Well, we have a job on this morning, but will this afternoon do?"

At this point Paul whispered that Dandylion would be tired, but Lucien only said, "Ssssh."

Major Davis said that this afternoon would do, if the manager was the sort of man who kept his word, but, judging from his personal experience, very few people in the Scholar's Water district were in the habit of keeping their words.

Lucien replied, "I can assure you, sir, that this is a very reliable firm and will not let you down. We will be at your house between two and half-past."

Major Davis said, "Good," and then they both rang off.

"An excellent half-hour's work," remarked Lucien, turning to Paul, who said, "I hope you kept the morning clear."

"Why? Oh, of course, I haven't told you about Mrs. Saunders, have I? You were outside."

"No, but I've fixed us up for this morning. I've arranged for us to take a trunk to the station."

"But you can't have. I've arranged for us to window clean. When did you arrange it?"

"Ten minutes ago!"

"Why didn't you tell any one?"

"Why didn't *you* tell any one about *your* window cleaning?"

"You were all outside. I was going to tell you when you came in."

"Well, I had only just put down the receiver when that Major Thing-a-me-jig rang up. I tried to get your attention when you were speaking to him, but you only said 'Ssssh' in a most irritating way."

"Now, what on earth are we going to do? We can't possibly put either of them off. What time did you say we would be along for the trunk? If you just said the morning, perhaps we could do the windows first."

"I said we would be along right away. We've got to put it on the eleven-ten Birmingham train, you see."

Lucien groaned, "We'll have to get a move on then. I suppose you and Marie had better take the trunk and Jennet and Sheila come with me. We won't look a very impressive window-cleaning gang. Where is Marie, by the way?"

"Gone to Bullit's to get some golden syrup for Tibbles."

"Is the trunk a large one?"

"I don't know."

"Didn't you ask?"

"No. I don't know really why we are fussing. After all there are seven of us. Surely we can manage two jobs at once. I think we've made a jolly good start. We're certainly in demand. It's lucky we are such a large family."

"Tibbles doesn't think so," remarked Jennet, entering from the garden with straw in her hair, wearing tattered dungarees and a yellow pullover. "She says if there were only three of us, Daddy could buy us ponies and canoes and Lucien a shotgun."

"Tibbles isn't always right," said Paul.

"Oh, she *is*—at least *nearly* always," contradicted Jennet, who was particularly fond of the old nurse.

"After all, if Paul and Marie find the trunk is too heavy they can get a porter," Lucien thought aloud.

"What is all this about windows and trunks?" asked Jennet.

"You explain, Lucien, please," said Paul.

So Lucien told Jennet about the window cleaning, the trunk and the mower. And Jennet leaped up and down and said, "But, it's marvellous. We'll make pounds—pounds and pounds. We'll soon be able to buy a pony. Perhaps, in a month or two, we'll be bidding at Tatterstall's for a nice pony of 14.2, which can just carry Lucien and is all right for the twins—not that they matter so much, as they can ride Dandylion."

"Thank you very much, I don't want to be *just carried*," said Lucien, but Jennet did not hear, because she was running out of the house to tell Sheila, Lottie and Charles about the telephone calls. As usual, she didn't look where she was going and tripped over a bucket, which Paul had left in the middle of the path after feeding Flippy and Flappy. She cut her knee on a small flint and sat clasping it, muttering, "How silly, oh dear, how very silly," for some moments, before rising and running to find Sheila digging in her little patch of garden by the old pigsty. And

23

Sheila wouldn't listen to Jennet's gabbled information, but merely pointed out that Jennet's spectacles were about to fall off and that her knee was bleeding and ought to be washed. "You'll get tetanus if you get earth in that cut," said Sheila. "Remember Bennet's horse died of it."

"Do you mean lockjaw?" asked Jennet in horror.

"Yes. Come on; if Tibbles catches you with a knee like that she'll be furious."

"We must be quick, because we've got to go window cleaning," said Jennet, and, on their way back to the house, she told Sheila what had happened.

Meanwhile, Marie came running back from Bullit's with the golden syrup under her arm, yelling, "Hoi, hoi! Lucien, Sheila, Paul, Jennet, twins! Good news. Come quickly, Hoi! Here!"

And, hearing her calls, the Pennyfield children had soon all come into the dining-room. "Well, spit it out," said Jennet.

"I've fixed us up with a job this morning—fifteen windows to clean at the Vicarage and I've promised to be there by a quarter past eleven and the Reverend Lucas says he is going to recommend us to all his friends and he's sure Doctor Heath and Doctor Whitby will want us to clean *their* windows. Isn't it amazing! I nearly jumped for joy."

"What a catastrophe!" exclaimed Lottie.

"Aren't you pleased?" asked Marie, looking at the glum faces of her brothers and sisters.

"It's enough to drive a person mad—stark staring mad. Why must everything happen at the same moment. Now we are done for. Goodness knows what we're going to do. I don't," said Lucien.

"It's really very funny," said Jennet.

"It's a catastrophe," said Lottie.

"I suppose it won't alter the fate of nations, although it seems to us like a major tragedy," remarked Paul, who sometimes showed an amazingly good sense of proportion.

"What *is* the matter? I thought you would all be awfully pleased," said Marie, sounding and looking crestfallen.

"You might explain, Lucien," said Paul. "I've forgotten the mower man's name."

So, for the third time in half an hour, Lucien explained about the jobs they had promised to take on for Mrs. Saunders, Miss Parker and Major Davis.

"It seems as though we've got to break one of our promises and I only said down the telephone this morning that we were a reliable firm," Lucien finished dismally.

"It comes of being a large family. Never mind, I don't expect old man Lucas would make a fuss if we rang him up and let him know we were not coming," said Jennet cheerfully.

"Listen," said Paul. "If we don't start off with Dandylion very soon we won't catch the train with that trunk and I'm not going to break my word for any one."

"I'm going to clean the Vicar's windows, whatever happens," said Marie.

"Do let's be sensible," suggested Lucien. "The trunk is obviously the most urgent job. We can't do both lots of windows at once, because we haven't got enough ladders. Did Lucas say he was in any particular hurry? Mrs. Saunders has got a party this evening."

"No, I offered to get his windows done this morning and he was *so* pleased. He said he could see at once that we were a truly efficient and prompt firm."

"I'm going to catch Dandylion," said Paul, leaving the room.

"I'll help," shouted Lottie, dashing after him.

"One lot of windows will have to be done this afternoon, which is it to be?" asked Lucien.

"Surely, Marie, it would be quite simple for you to ring up the Reverend Lucas and explain that, while you were out, your brother had fixed up another engagement for the Window Cleaning Service. You could say that you had no idea that we would have so many people wanting us at once," said Sheila.

"I hate letting people down," said Marie obstinately.

"That sounds priggish. It won't hurt his windows to wait until this afternoon. If we are going to be punctual, we haven't much timet o collect our ladders and things before starting for Mrs. Saunders' house," said Jennet.

"I don't mind whether it sounds priggish or not, but, if the *Scholar Farm Quick Window Cleaning Service* is to have a good reputation, it ought to keep its word."

"Don't you understand, Marie?" said Lucien. "Mrs. Saunders' windows must be done, because she's holding a party to-night. The Vicar can surely wait until three or four this afternoon. He didn't say he wanted them done quickly; you offered and he was pleased, because it was such a change after all the frustration and hold-ups of present-day life. I'm certain he won't mind; after all, he's an educated and intelligent man and is sure to have a sense of proportion. I'll ring up now and explain the difficulty. Do you think some of you could possibly collect some swabs and buckets and dusters." He ran out of the room, wondering how three people could clean ten windows in two hours and a half.

As he picked up the telephone receiver, he heard Tibbles scolding Charles, "I've told you time and again not to spill oats on the bathroom floor, but, so far as I can see, I might as well speak to that there wall as speak to you, for it's not a bit of use, not a bit. Now go downstairs and get the dustpan and brush . . ." The nurse's voice trailed away.

"Hallo, Lucien Pennyfield speaking. Is that the Reverend Lucas?" asked Lucien.

Chapter Four

HALF AN HOUR later Sheila, Paul, Dandylion and Brockie were jogging down the wet road to Thrushfield.

"How wonderful everything smells after the shower," said Paul, "and all the fields seem to be smiling. I do love April."

"I wish Marie hadn't been so determined to go window cleaning," said Sheila. "She's much better at managing Dandylion than I am."

"She's cross, because her arrangements have been spoilt, and I don't blame her. Lucas is much nicer than Mrs. Saunders, who wears such awfully long frocks and is so dim and dowdy."

"Don't be beastly," said Sheila, thinking that it was odd that a dreamy inattentive boy of ten like Paul should never fail to notice when someone was badly dressed, when their clothes were too long or their colours clashed. All the more odd, because Paul never cared much about his own appearance, would often annoy Tibbles by going into Kingham wearing his oldest and most disreputable coat, which was holely at the elbows and had belonged to Lucien before it belonged to Paul.

Now he said, "It's not beastly, there's no need for her to dress like that. She's quite well off and I bet her clothes are expensive; she's just got no taste."

"And so she shouldn't have her windows cleaned first," said Sheila. "I say, I hope we can lift the trunk. I wish Marie was here; she's so much stronger than I am. We haven't decided how much to charge yet."

"Oh, not much," said Paul. "About two bob, I should think."

"I don't agree. Considering Kingham is four miles from Thrushfield, I should say at least three and six."

"Oh *no*!" exclaimed Paul, who was perhaps the least mercenary of the Pennyfields—if any of them could be described as truly mercenary. When he had anything to sell, Paul always asked a ridiculously low sum and, having a horror of beating people down or haggling, he was frequently *done*—much to the disgust of Tibbles, Butt (the charlady) and Jennet.

Now he was very put out by Sheila's suggestion. "Three and sixpence! Just for taking a trunk. Why, I was thinking two bob was too much. The return bus fare is only one and tuppence."

"But it's going to take nearly the whole morning and we've got to put it on the train and probably sign something. I'm sure Marie would charge five shillings if she was here."

"All right. I don't mind," said Paul, always loath to argue. "It probably won't ruin Miss Parker anyway, and I don't expect we'll get a reputation for overcharging. She didn't sound a talkative kind of woman—rather meek, I should think."

"Three and six is *not* overcharging," contradicted Sheila. "The others will be furious if we ask less. Oh dear, I hope we are not going to be late. I wish I had thought of

27

borrowing Marie's watch. *Do* hurry up, Dandylion."

They jogged on slowly, in spite of Sheila's words. The donkey always played up these two drivers. Lucien could get her along by using the whip skilfully, Marie by threats, Lottie by slapping her with her hands, Charles by calling her names. But Sheila—the meekest of the Pennyfields—was always afraid that the little grey donkey might be tired and so only urged her in a half-hearted manner, which had no effect at all. Paul, on the other hand, practically never had any wish to hurry; he liked to read as he drove or to look at the landscape and, as soon as he took over the reins, Dandylion took it for granted that she might dawdle. Jennet, she knew, was all fingers and thumbs, and she knew that, if she turned round or backed into a ditch, Jennet would either drop the reins or lose her spectacles, so with her, also, she behaved as she pleased.

"It is tiresome," Sheila remarked now. "I do wish I could make her behave; yet I'm sure she's not really lazy. Do you think the cart's too heavy. Perhaps one of us ought to get out. I'm sure we're going to be late."

"I don't think the cart's too heavy, because she simply raced along when Lottie was driving the other day and it had three people in it then *and* two dogs."

"That was on the way home and she's quite different then. Would you like to have a try?"

"No, I shan't be any better. Hit her with the reins—hard."

"All right," said Sheila, and she leaned forward and flicked the donkey twice sharply with the reins. "Oh dear, I'm sure I hurt her," she said.

"There's the church clock striking ten," remarked Paul quite calmly. "Can you hit her any harder? I'm sure she's getting slower and slower."

He was right; the donkey was beginning to walk every now and then and her eyes were on the side of the road; she was looking for a nice mouthful of grass.

"*You* hit her then, instead of telling me what to do," said Sheila.

"All right."

Paul seized the end of the reins and, leaning forward, struck her three times between the collar and the pad.

Without any warning Dandylion stopped, and it was so sudden that Paul fell right out of the cart into a puddle on the side of the road.

"Oh gosh!" exclaimed Sheila, leaping out. "Are you all right?"

"Yes, quite, thank you. My clothes are rather wet, but it's of no consequence." Paul spoke in the voice he always used when he was upset or nearly in tears. He said things were of no consequence more to convince himself than his companions on these occasions.

"Oh dear. Tibbles will be cross," said Sheila.

"I don't mind about Tibbles. I shall be dry by the time I get home. It's Miss Parker I'm thinking about."

"Well, look, take off your coat. There, your shirt's hardly damp and, if you lurk in the background, she won't notice your seat. For goodness' sake, hurry up."

"I'm cold without a coat. I'll run in front of Dandylion until I'm warm. Perhaps it will hurry her up."

Sheila turned Brockie out and so they continued, with Paul and the dog running ahead; and the donkey seemed to go faster now. They arrived at Miss Parker's house at nine minutes past ten. A maid in a cap and apron—an unusual sight in Thrushfield—opened the door, exclaimed in horror when Sheila explained her errand and said that Madam had been expecting a car.

Paul said that, so far as he could see, it was of no consequence whether a donkey or a car took the trunk, so long as it reached the station in time; and Sheila looked extremely worried and asked the maid to tell them where their cargo was, as soon as possible.

The maid said, "Doubt if you can lift it. Madam was expecting a man—not a couple of kids."

Paul said, "A tough young man *was* coming; only he was stopped at the last moment by unforeseen circumstances. Such is Fate."

Sheila said, "Where is the trunk, please? We've no time to waste," and Paul added, "We must be quick."

The maid said, "I should say so, with that old donkey."

So Paul replied, "She's not old, or anyway she's a jolly sight younger than you are."

The maid, who had just entered middle age, when,

29

according to Lucien, people take the greatest pains to look younger than their years, was obviously annoyed by this remark and muttered, "None of your sauce," angrily, as she took them round to the back door. Sheila nudged Paul and whispered, "Tactless," and at the same time realised, with horror, that they should have never gone to the front door in the first place. She felt very miserable at this moment but the sight of the trunk cheered her up, for it was neither very large or very heavy and she had expected it to be both.

"Oh gosh! That's nothing," said Paul, sounding as though he was very strong indeed.

The maid helped them round, explaining on the way that Madam was in bed and that it was extremely important for the trunk to get on the train.

Dandylion was tactlessly eating a shrub in the drive and Brockie was putting the contents of the dustbin on the gravel. Paul apologised for both the animals' bad behaviour; then the two children jumped into the cart with the trunk and, thanking the maid, who, odd though it may seem, appeared to be laughing, jogged away down the drive. For a few moments Dandylion thought she was going home and condescended to trot quite fast, but all too soon they turned off for Kingham and then she dropped back to her old pace of about three miles an hour.

Paul passed a dirty mud-stained hand through his thick hair. "We're going to be late," he said.

"What can we do?" wondered Sheila.

"I know what that maid was laughing at—my wet clothes," said Paul.

After this remark, they were both silent for several minutes; they were both wondering how they could possibly get the trunk to Kingham by ten minutes past eleven. Suddenly Paul said:

"I've got it."

"Got what?" asked Sheila.

"An idea; wait a moment and you will see what it is," Paul told her; and then he sprang out of the cart and walked beside the meandering Dandylion, pausing to look behind him every now and then. A small car full of children passed and a motor bike and a larger car with a chauffeur and then a lorry came along, missing on one cylinder, and Paul ran into the middle of the road, put out both arms and yelled, "Whoa, please." The driver looked surprised, but he stopped and called, "What's up, sonny?"

"We're in a fix," explained Paul, "wanted to catch the eleven-ten to Birmingham with this trunk and now our donkey's turned temperamental and won't hurry and it's half-past ten and we've still got four miles to go; so I wondered whether you could give one of us and the trunk a lift; that is, if you're going to Kingham."

Paul's voice trailed away; he had suddenly lost courage, was afraid that he was really being an awful nuisance. Sheila, who hated asking a favour of any one, although she liked to help people out of difficulties herself, felt embarrassed and was silent.

It seemed an age before the lorry driver answered. In fact Paul was about to hop in the cart and trot away, so sure was he that the man was annoyed, when at last the answer came.

"All right, sonny, jump in; and 'and 'in the trunk, miss. I'm not by rights going into Kingham, but I dare say I could run you down to the station."

"Oh, thanks," said Paul, "thanks awfully."

"It's most frightfully kind of you. I do hope it is not too much trouble," said Sheila.

"You 'and up that trunk, miss, and don't worry your 'ead about the trouble," ordered the lorry man.

Sheila did as she was bid, and a few moments later Paul was whizzing along the main road to Kingham, feeling very pleased with himself; he had never been in a lorry before and he did not notice that this one was old or that it missed on one cylinder. He tried to talk to the driver, but the noise in the cab was so great that conversation was rather difficult and then he noticed that the driver's ears were filled with cotton wool, and after that he gave up.

When they reached the station at five minutes to eleven, Paul wanted to tip the driver, but, feeling in his pockets, he found he had only either half a crown or a threepenny bit. This made him feel very awkward, because he thought threepence would be much too little and yet, if he gave the

31

"We're in a fix," explained Paul.

half-crown, he would have nothing left to pay for the trunk.

He hovered and wished that he had thought of asking Sheila to give him some money, and turned the coins over in his hands. Then he dropped them and that seemed to make matters much worse. The driver looked at them as they lay on the ground—or so it seemed to Paul—as though he thought he ought to have a tip (actually, he was wondering whether two shillings and ninepence would be enough to pay for a trunk to go to Birmingham). Paul felt himself grow hot and felt himself grow cold and then, after what seemed like an age, but was really only fifty seconds, he picked up the money, and saying, "Well, thank you very much for all your trouble, thank you very much indeed," handed the driver the half-crown.

The driver, who was very slow in the uptake, stared at him for a moment, before saying: "Don't you worry about that, sonny; it was no trouble; you're welcome. You'll be needing that money for the railway; you've got to pay in advance nowadays and you'd better 'urry up or you'll be missing that train."

Then, suddenly, it dawned on him that Paul couldn't possibly lift the trunk by himself and that there was no porter in sight. Handing back the half-crown, he leapt out of his lorry, seized the trunk and said, "Come on, now, or we'll never get it on in time." And in another moment they were on the platform and then he was talking persuasively to the guard and then everything was fixed and he lent Paul fivepence, because the charge had been three shillings and twopence. Paul wanted him to wait until Sheila turned up, but he wouldn't; he said he had another hundred miles to go before lunch and that Paul could forget it, so Paul was unable to pay him back; and, as he sat on the edge of a porter's trunk, just outside the station, he decided that the driver was a jolly nice man and that it must be rather fun to go all across England in a lorry. If I'm not a good poet, he thought, I shall go into the transport trade. Then he composed a poem:

33

I should never be sorry
To go in a lorry,
And drive all through the day.
I think it is fun,
But not every one
Looks at it in the same way.

You whizz through the land
And can lend a hand,
To a person who's stuck on the road.
In summer and spring
You see everything
And you're always changing abode.

You wear wool in your ears,
But don't worry, my dears!
It isn't because of a pain;
Just the grunting and groans
And terrible moans
Of the lorry's a bit of a strain.

He was thinking about the fourth verse, when he saw Sheila coming across the station yard; she was pulling Dandylion with one hand and leading Brockie with the other. The three of them and the little cart looked like farmyard toys. Some boys loitering at the roadside chanted, "I 'ad a donkey and it wouldn't go." Several shoppers, mostly women with children, exclaimed, "Oh, how sweet!" Sheila did not appear as though she shared their opinion. As she came nearer, Paul noticed that she wore a harassed expression and that she looked as though she had been dragging Dandylion for at least a mile. Her usually tidy hair was hanging over her face and her blouse, a school one, had parted from her brown tweed skirt, leaving a gap which showed her vest. She looked more like Lottie than Sheila.

"Hallo!" yelled Paul and she didn't answer, and he knew that this was because she did not want to call any more attention to herself; for Sheila was not an exhibitionist like Jennet and Lottie; she shared Tibbles' dislike of being noticed and hated making a fool of herself. But

Brockie heard and, being fond of Paul, he danced and yapped and nearly pulled Sheila over, so Paul ran, dodging through the traffic, and helped his sister turn the cart round and then the two of them, the dog and the donkey started for home.

Paul told Sheila about everything except his attempt at tipping, which he thought she might think silly. She liked his poem, but said that he wouldn't like being a lorry driver really, because he would have to eat sausage meat and black pudding at transport cafés and he would never have enough blankets on his bed in the different abodes. Then she told him of her difficulties, how Dandylion *would* stop to graze; how Brockie *would* jump out of the cart and run across the road; how an obliging farm labourer helped her. While she talked, the donkey, pleased to be going home at last, trotted briskly between the tall thorn hedges, which line the Thrushfield road. Far away, a church clock struck the single hour.

"We'll be late for lunch," said Paul.

"Oh dear, Tibbles *will* be cross," said Sheila; "she's made an apple pudding."

Chapter Five

THAT evening in the nursery the Pennyfields counted the takings of the day. . . .

"Ten shillings from Mrs. Saunders, two shillings for the mower and eight shillings from the Reverend Lucas—a pound; that's not bad for the first day and then, of course, there's the trunk money, three and sixpence, to come in. Are you writing out the bill, Sheila? Don't forget to add the railway fare," said Lucien.

"I'm not likely to," she replied. "We must all carry more money with us in future. It really was *awful*, Paul having to be given money by that driver and such a bad advertisement."

"I think it must have been rather funny. You're much too good," said Jennet.

"A catastrophe," said Lottie.

"Do stop making such a fuss. It won't end the world if I was given some money. The driver's probably laughed about it ever since," said Paul, who was sick and tired of hearing about the episode.

"And it was awful, too—you telling that lie, about the strong young man being prevented from coming, to the maid," Sheila went on undaunted. "Besides, telling lies being wrong, every one will expect the transport service to take on heavy jobs."

"Lucien's strong and at sixteen you count as a young man," muttered Paul.

"Major Davis thought us a joke," remarked Jennet, with the air of someone who is averting an argument.

"I must say, I was very apprehensive about that mower. I thought he had every right to be angry when he found we were not a gang of men and I was really surprised when he said we were enterprising and charged too little," said Lucien.

"Let's decide about to-morrow," suggested Marie. "The twins will have to go to bed in a minute."

"Oh no! Don't be horrid," wailed Lottie.

"Tibbles will be calling for you," their eldest sister went on ruthlessly. "The Reverend Lucas has got three windows to be cleaned. Sheila, you want to send off an advertisement about typing, don't you? Lottie wants to practise for the circus. Charles wants to paint a tub; so it looks as though Lucien, Paul, Jennet and I had better go."

"I shall probably break a window," said Paul gloomily.

"Don't be silly," said Jennet sharply. "Anyway, it won't end the world if you do. Old Lucas was jolly nice; he sent out a tray of chocolate biscuits and lemonade and he was awfully agreeable. He's not the sort of person to care about broken windows. He told me he was awfully bad in youth. I should come, honestly I should."

"Jennet, you're frightful," said Sheila. "And the Vicar's not *old*. But I don't think many of us can go, because Tibbles says we are to lend a hand in the house. Apparently, Paul and Lottie didn't make their beds yesterday and that's annoyed her."

"*I* did all the breakfast washing up yesterday," said Lottie.

36

"Oh, you *didn't*. I helped like anything," contradicted Jennet.

"I told Lucas we would probably arrive at about eleven, so surely we can all help Tibbles before we start," suggested Lucien.

"I'm going to peel some potatoes now," declared Jennet leaving the room.

"Right-o. That's agreed—we'll help in the house early in the morning," said Marie, as though she was glad that something was settled at last.

"Think how awful it would have been if Jennet had been Paul yesterday—she had nothing in her pocket, not a sou. I do think if we shared out some of to-day's takings and each carried half a crown, it would be a help. I mean there would be less likelihood of us getting into fixes and having to ask to be given money," said Sheila, harking back to her old suggestion.

"I did *not* ask to be given money. He plonked fivepence down before I realised what had happened and if you had been a bit quicker I might have paid him back," said Paul angrily.

"Yes," said Lucien, "although half a crown was not enough for Paul to-day, it might often save the situation."

"It will be useful for bribing people to be quiet when Dandylion misbehaves, bumps into a car or backs into a shop window or anything. Has anybody seen the little sharp knife?" said Jennet, reappearing.

"No," answered Marie decisively.

"Try under the draining board," suggested Lucien.

"Wait a sec!" interrupted Marie. "Let's share out the money now. Here's half a crack, Jennet; don't lose it; it's supposed to be kept for emergencies, so don't spend it unless you absolutely have to."

"I will see if Tibbles can change this ten-bob note," said Lucien.

"Please don't fetch her now or she'll make us go to bed," said the twins.

Their plea was in vain, for at that moment the nurse appeared and cried, "Come along, you tiresome children; you should have been in bed long ago. What your poor father would say if he was here, I can't think."

37

"Quick, here's your money," said Lucien, and the twins, who couldn't remember when they last had so much money, went to bed quite meekly.

The other Pennyfields stayed up later. Lucien started an article on ferreting for the magazine. Marie tried to type a short story on her father's typewriter. Sheila wrote to a man called Hopkins, who was advertising bee-hives in the *Smallholder's Monthly*.

Jennet returned, after hacking the peel off twenty potatoes, and drafted a programme of her variety show, on which, having cut her thumb with the little sharp knife, she subsequently bled. Paul wrote a short poem, which started:

When you are weary and all the world seems black,
And you have taken money and cannot pay it back,
And your companions linger on your unruly act,
Break from reality, cast the thought aside,
Let your mind wander, on imagination ride
To some beauteous spot, some pleasant heaven. . . .

But, on reading these lines through, he was dissatisfied and he tore the whole poem up before going to bed.

Lucien and Marie were the last to follow him. Before having their baths, they discussed the twins. Marie said they should not be allowed to come on window-cleaning expeditions, because: (*a*) They gave an unprofessional air to the gang; (*b*) They would, sooner or later, break a window; (*c*) They made such a row and trod on the borders.

Lucien said they should be allowed to come, because: (*a*) It was horrible to be always left at home; (*b*) They were often useful at wringing out leathers and passing up dusters; (*c*) It was easier for Tibbles if they were out of her way.

When Lucien and Marie eventually got into their beds, they were still undecided on the subject.

Next morning dawned bright and clear and, after trying to help Tibbles for nearly an hour, the window-cleaning party set off whistling gaily and carrying numerous buckets, two ladders and the usual dusters, leathers and rags.

Lottie dashed out to the orchard with half a loaf of bread, caught Dandylion and started to teach her to lie down. Charles found a beer barrel by the coal hole, but no paint, and retired in disgust to read *Mrs. Tittlemouse*, which he had already read three times. Sheila drafted an advertisement for *The Kingham Chronicle*, starting: *Typing Taken*, and then took the dogs for a walk to the Post Office and lost Brockie, the wire-haired terrier, who went off after rabbits.

Lottie soon tired of trying to make Dandylion lie down and removed the dog collar, which she had tied round one of the donkey's forelegs, and practised riding facing the tail and standing on her head, until she had fallen off five times and felt quite dizzy. Then she gave Dandylion the rest of the bread and sat on the granary steps, and started to make a set of harness for Tock by plaiting garden twine.

Discussing their morning's activities at lunch, every one except Charles felt that they had helped the cause, although Lucien and Marie were disappointed because nobody had rung up and asked for their services.

It was only after lunch that Lottie found, to her horror, that she had lost her half-crown. With growing trepidation, she helped finish the washing up before running out to search the orchard, for she felt certain that she must have lost it while practising for the circus. How easily the coin could have fallen out of the pocket of her shorts when she stood on her head, or fell from Dandylion into the lush spring grass. She felt furious with herself and, as the moments passed and she was unable to find the half-crown, the thought of telling the others of her stupidity seemed to become more and more impossible. At last, she gave up the search and found and told Charles the sad story. He agreed that it was a serious catastrophe and suggested that they should earn half a crown and pay back the money before nightfall.

"It seems terrible," said Lottie. "The others have taken so much trouble to earn three bob this morning and I just throw away two and sixpence."

"Well, you didn't throw it away on purpose; but I must

39

say I could have done with it for paint; but never mind, we can soon make some money, even though we are only eight. I don't see why the others should do all the earning anyway."

"We could go from door to door asking every one if they want any weeding done, couldn't we?" suggested Lottie.

"Or any letters posted," added Charles.

"Seems a bit like begging," ventured Lottie. "Sheila would say it was a bad advertisement."

"I wish we were in France. Daddy says the children there get paid for watching the sheep and cows grazing at the roadside; I expect they can read at the same time, too; and it's not so back-aching as weeding. I've got an idea! What about chopping some lighting wood and selling it in bundles? We could soon earn half a crown like that."

"No one wants to buy wood in the summer and Tibbles says we are not to use the chopper. Begging or no begging, let's try to get some weeding to do—*Nothing venture, nothing win*—isn't that what Marie says?" asked Lottie.

"I think so; but weeding makes my arms ache," replied Charles.

"Oh, don't be such a grandfather. Come on; let's go before someone stops us. We had better take a dog. Tibbles says it is not so bad us going out on our own if we've got one with us."

Ten minutes later, with no definite plan, the twins set out in the direction of Scholar's Water. Lottie carried Sheila's trowel and Charles her little fork. "Makes us look more processional," Lottie said—meaning *professional*. They were accompanied by a very unwilling Cockade. A light wind blew gently in their faces; far away in the sky clouds were rolling up from the west, threatening rain.

Charles produced his mouth organ and tried to play "Daisy, Daisy, Give Me Your Answer, Do," which Lottie said sounded most unprocessional. They had a slight argument over this and then Charles suddenly cried, "Lottie, look! Just look at all those weeds." And they came to an abrupt halt. To the left of them was a small glaring house, with an ugly stony garden fenced by barbed wire; and in this garden was a circular drive, which had once been gravel, but was now green with weeds. There were plantains and groundsel, couch grass and clover, ground elder and dandelions and an occasional poppy, and these did not keep only to the drive, but spread over the little stony borders and even clustered underneath the windows, which were bow-fronted and very hideous.

"No one can want their garden to look like that. But oh, how horrible and ugly it all is!" exclaimed Charles, returning his mouth organ to the pocket of his coat, where, unknown to Lottie, Tick was lurking.

"It's queer that we haven't noticed the house before. I don't know why we don't come down this lane more often."

"Marie told me the other day that it was because someone was murdered here just before the war and it gives Tibbles the creeps," replied Charles.

"Oh dear," said Lottie, feeling a shiver run down her spine. "Come on; let's bang at the door."

"What shall we say?"

"Would you like us to do some weeding?"

"Who's going to say it?"

"Me, I suppose—if you are afraid."

"I'm *not* afraid."

"Well, *you*, then."

"Why should I?"

"Oh, don't be silly, Charles. I believe you *are* frightened."

"I'm *not*. We can both say it."

"All right; come on."

"You go first, Lottie, because I've got Cockade."

"Bags bang at the door. What an awful knocker. Won't it be a catastrophe if there's no one in?"

"Yes," said Charles, secretly wishing he wasn't here at all. Lottie's bang seemed to resound right through the house and then they heard footsteps and, a moment later, the door was opened by a little man with a large nose and very black hair.

"Good morning," said Lottie.

"Good afternoon," said Charles at the same time. And then for a few seconds the twins looked confused; before both bursting into speech again. "Would you like your garden weeded?" they asked, and the little man smiled and suddenly Lottie noticed that his nose was very like a beak and she laughed, and he said, "Pardon?" Lottie gave Charles a glance which meant *don't speak at the same time*, and repeated, "Would you like your garden weeded?" And then, at last, the little man understood and answered that he would very much, thank you.

"We'll start right away then," Charles told him, trying to sound efficient.

"There's plenty to do," said Lottie, looking at the drive with an unintentionally disapproving air.

"Yes, young lady, there certainly is; you won't get it clear in a few hours." The man made a noise which seemed to Charles to be half a cackle and half a laugh. Lottie wondered why a weedy garden was funny; but soon found that this dark little man laughed at almost everything—indeed whenever he spoke. "I suppose you are wanting to make a bit of brass?" he asked now, in teasing accents.

"Not brass—*money*—half a crown actually," said Charles.

The man cackled and laughed again and Lottie, who did not know that *brass* was a north-country expression for *money*, thought he was very irritating. She made a dab at a poppy with Sheila's trowel and said, "Can we begin now, please?"

"Certainly, certainly. You'll find it a back-aching job, though. Does your mother know what you are up to?"

"Our mother is dead," said Charles very firmly. "So I expect she might see us from heaven."

"Tibbles says it is possible," added Lottie.

"Tch, tch," said the little dark man, actually not laughing as he spoke. "Well, you start away, children; get the weeds up by the roots and stick to the drive to-day, and presently I'll come and see how you are getting on."

He disappeared into the house and Lottie exclaimed, "Hurray, hurray! We are going to earn some money at last."

"I think he was jolly decent. Do you think he will pay us half a crown?" Charles wondered.

"I don't like him," said Lottie, kneeling down in the drive. "He's strange."

"Oh, he *isn't*. He's very agreeable—look how he kept laughing. . . ."

For nearly half an hour the twins worked without another word passing between them; and then, as Charles tugged at the roots of a dandelion, Tick suddenly jumped out of his pocket and scuttled away in some couch grass.

"Oh, Charles! Why *did* you bring him?" cried Lottie.

"Quick! You silly idiot—why didn't you grab him?" screeched Charles.

Frantically, they searched on hands and knees, but, although they saw Tick occasionally, he always managed to evade them and disappear into the grass again, until he reached a strip of nearly weedless gravel at the back of the house and then he streaked across it in full view and went into a new-looking shed.

"Oh gosh! " cried Charles.

"Oh quick; he's getting behind some boxes," shouted Lottie. The twins plunged inside and Charles threw himself down behind a large galvanised bin, which was firmly padlocked and all but grabbed the little white mouse.

"Tick, Tick; come on, Tick," called Lottie. "Oh, Charles, you are slow. Where's he gone now?"

"By those trunks and gosh don't they smell! "

"Like a hen-house, but then this shed looks as though it might have been made as a big hen-house."

And now a figure darkened the doorway—it was the little man with a large nose and he looked very angry. Lottie noticed, for the first time, that his eyes seemed small and hard. Both twins felt incredibly and unreasonably guilty.

"Sorry," said Charles.

"We couldn't help stopping—it's our mouse, you see. He's escaped from a pocket and bolted in here. He's white. I suppose you can't see him anywhere; we are all awfully bad at looking," Lottie explained.

Their employer appeared to make a supreme effort to control his anger and, when he spoke, his tone was quite pleasant.

"Just you two come outside for a moment and clear the boards and I'll find your mouse for you. I've got very sharp eyes and I'm quick on my feet too," he said.

Looking very relieved, the twins said, "Oh, *thank you*" —for both of them hated searching for anything—and came out and stood in the garden. The little man cackled and laughed for no apparent reason and, after shutting himself in the shed, made coaxing noises and shifted boxes about, occasionally whistling some refrain.

"Do you think we ought to go back to our weeding?" Lottie asked Charles.

"He said he would only be a moment, so I expect we're supposed to wait."

"I hope the others are not wondering where we are. We ought to have left a note. Tibbles is sure to be fussing. My tummy says it's long past teatime. I do wish he would hurry if he's going to catch Tick. I can't see why we can't help; it would be much easier with three people."

"I expect he thinks we will trip over each other's feet. I wonder what the time is. I don't see why Tibbles need worry about us. She must know that we are old enough to look after ourselves."

"Listen, let's go and look through the kitchen window. I thought I saw a clock there."

"I don't want to go prying around. Can't we stand in the road and stop a bicyclist and ask the time."

"Then if *he* does catch Tick, he'll think we've gone home and kill him. People never think mice are worth anything. I believe you are frightened of him. Anyhow, it's not prying to look through a kitchen window at a clock."

"I'm not frightened."

"Well, come on, then."

Lottie led the way and, as there wasn't a clock in the kitchen, they looked through what appeared to be the sitting-room window, where a blue alarm clock sat amongst a mass of papers on an open writing-desk, saying half-past four. As they stared at the luminous green hands, they heard footsteps behind them and turned again to see an angry face with hard eyes and large beak-like nose.

"What are you looking for now?" he asked in accusing accents, and Charles replied meekly, "I am so sorry; we were trying to see the time."

44

"Did you manage to catch Tick?" Lottie thought it best to change the subject.

"If you mean the mouse, here he is, and I suggest you take him off as soon as possible, before he causes any more trouble."

Lottie was handed Tick and she shoved him in her pocket and then both twins were so struck by the man's anger, which seemed so unreasonable, that they forgot all about their half-crown, and shouting, "Sorry to be a nuisance," hurried to the front drive, collected Cockade, who was still patiently sitting tied to the gate and, without a thought for the fork and trowel, walked out into the road slamming the gate.

"He *did* look disagreeable. I said it was prying. I knew he would be cross. I believe he was cross with us for being in the shed," Charles grumbled.

"And all our work for nothing—nothing. Horrid stingy man—as if it hurt him, for us to look at the time."

"I think he just forgot about paying us. I mean he did mean to give us something at the beginning. Then he was so angry and we shot off so jolly quickly that he hadn't much chance to remember. I can't see why you wanted to tear away like that."

"I wasn't frightened: it was just that we seemed such a nuisance and he said we were to take Tick off as soon as possible and I didn't stop to think. If I had remembered I would have mentioned it. Oh dear, the others will be cross. What a beastly day it has been."

All the way home the twins worried about their reception; they were certain that their brothers and sisters would be furious that the half-crown should have been lost and the afternoon wasted in useless toil; and they were certain that Tibbles would be sick with worry, because of their lateness. They guessed that they would be sent to bed—not without tea though, for Tibbles believed in children eating as much food as possible. They had reached the footpath, which is the shortest way, if you are walking, from the Scholar's Water Road to Scholar's Farm, when they remembered Sheila's trowel and fork and the thought of these tools lying in the weedy drive sunk them in yet deeper gloom.

It was twilight when, in dismal silence, they climbed the last stile; the weather-cock on the barn was pointing south-west, clouds chased one another across a sea of grey. But the twins did not see this nor Paul's ducks leaving the green pond, and, when they reached the garden gate they heard Tibbles calling and Lucien ringing the cow-bell, which their mother had brought home from Switzerland long ago.

"Now we are in for it," said Lottie.

Chapter Six

THE three eldest Pennyfields felt very despondent that evening; they had, with difficulty, controlled their anger when the twins arrived; for Tibbles' angry words were enough to make Lottie and Charles feel miserable for quite a long time and they knew that no one could have wanted to lose half a crown or spend all afternoon weeding a drive for nothing.

But when the rest of the family were in bed, as the long expected rain beat upon the nursery window panes and a fierce wind whistled round the house and Tibbles sat in her wicker-chair darning socks, they discussed the misdeeds of their younger brothers and sisters. For Lottie had not been the only one to waste the money, with which she had been entrusted. Some of the other Pennyfields had gone into Kingham to help Tibbles with the shopping and, while lagging behind his companions down a side street, Paul had seen a pathetic beggar holding out his cap, and, in a sudden fit of generosity, had given him the silver half-crown. It would not have been so bad, Marie had said, if the man had not been such a rascal; his eyes were bloodshot, his chin was unshaven and had obviously been neglected for several days; there was no doubt that he had a strong taste for drink and Paul's money would have been handed across some bar by now.

Jennet, as well as spending her half-crown, had added to the household expenses. Told to wait by the bus stop for the rest of the party, she had fallen in love with a

46

miserable-looking black and white kitten sitting in the window of a pet shop and, whipping out her money, she had walked boldly in and bought it without hesitation. The annoying part about Paul's and Jennet's silly behaviour was that they did not seem to regret it or realise that it was disheartening for the other people who had earned the money; they both exclaimed in horror when accused of being thoughtless and selfish. . . .

"He was a very old man and his eyes were all red. I'm sure they had something wrong with them, some terrible disease, and he looked starved and thin, and told me he had seven children to support. Besides, Daddy says you should always give money to beggars and I couldn't pass him by. Who knows? He might have been a starving poet —think of Francis—what's his name—Thompson." Paul, who was naturally romantic, defended himself.

"But she's so sweet and she looked so miserable in that cage. How can you say it was throwing money away? I think you are all as stingy as a lot of old misers. You will be jolly sorry when she has kittens and I sell them for vast sums," Jennet had cried, offering the ugly scruffy kitten bread and milk.

And so seven and sixpence had been lost to the cause in one day—enough to buy half a dozen young bantams or half a step-ladder or to pay for a small advertisement in the local paper—and all the Pennyfields went to bed in miserable tempers.

Next morning Paul wakened first and lying in bed watched the sun rise; for the room, which he shared with Charles, faced east. As he listened to the birds and gazed at the sky, golden fresh and beautiful as only an April sky can be, he thought of yesterday and the wretched unshaved beggar and gradually he composed a poem. It was this:

> As I lie, I see the sky
>   And the sun is rising red,
> And I sigh, and my mind's eye
>   Sees a beggar, underfed.
>
> Are you afoot yet, Beggar?
>   Are you alive and about?

Are you walking the streets, Beggar?
　Or haven't you ventured out?

Are you still asleep, Beggar?
　Lying askew on sacks,
Or have you really a house, Beggar?
　Or do you dream by the stacks?

Do you really tell lies, Beggar?
　Or is your family seven?
If your tales aren't true, Beggar,
　You won't reach heaven.

I gave you my half-crown, Beggar,
　It wasn't all for drink;
I meant some for food, Beggar,
　Which would be right, I think.

Your eyes looked bloodshot, Beggar,
　I thought you were going blind.
Marie says it's drink, Beggar,
　But I think she's being unkind.

Can you see the sun now, Beggar?
　Golden and round and red,
Or are you still asleep, Beggar?
　Or searching for food instead? . . .

Paul had scribbled these seven verses on the back of a
magazine in red chalk when Jennet came bursting into the
room.

"Flippy and Flappy," she gasped, "they've gone, gone.
I went to let them out and they weren't there." She stood
shivering in her pyjamas, for Jennet was inclined to venture out before dressing—generally to ride Dandylion—
much to Tibbles' consternation.

Paul was slow to collect his thoughts and take in her
tragic words. He sat dazed for a moment, his mind still
searching for rhymes, and then, suddenly, he realised all.

"But I shut them up," he cried. "I bolted the door.

You've made a mistake. You've been dreaming—that's it—dreaming."

"I *haven't*. I went out to practise Dandylion for the variety show, before Lottie gets up and tires her out. And they haven't got through the window, because I looked and it's shut. I tell you they've gone, gone."

"I'm going to look," said Paul more calmly now, because he was determined that his ducks could not have disappeared and he had noticed that Jennet was not wearing her spectacles, and every one who knew Jennet knew that she could never see anything without her spectacles. He put on the dark green corduroy dressing-gown, which had been Lucien's before it was his, and, barefooted, the two of them ran in silence to the orchard, where Paul's yellow duckhouse stood beneath the boughs of a little crooked apple tree. The door was open and sure enough there were no ducks within.

"I know they were here when I shut them up last night, because I had Tibbles' torch and I tried to make them eat a peppermint," he said, standing on one foot, because the grass was wet with early dew and his toes were cold.

"Let's search the orchard," yelled Jennet, hitching up her striped pyjamas, which used to belong to Paul and had been chosen by Tibbles.

"All right," said Paul miserably.

So they wandered in the wet grass, calling, and Jennet found a bucket and rattled it; but they found no ducks and, at last, seeing Tibbles at the passage window, they went indoors and Paul walked slowly upstairs and sat on his bed and cried, which wasn't so babyish as it sounds, because, after all, he was only ten.

Jennet soon spread the sad news round the house and in a few moments all his brothers and sisters were searching the orchard and garden and also the adjoining fields which belonged to their father, but had been let with the farm to Mr. Bennet.

It was a wonderful day. A clear golden sun shone from a sapphire sky and, after yesterday's rain, the whole landscape looked cleaner, fresher, lovelier; even the dark and dirty mud by the farm gate seemed quite pleasnt.

It seemed incredible to Paul, as he left the refuge of his

bedroom to join the others, that such a morning should be marred by such a tragedy as the disappearance of Flippy and Flappy. He thought the sun should fade in sorrow and the sky rain tears in sympathy; it seemed all wrong that the world should go on as usual.

"It would have been different if they had been old," he said at breakfast, "but they were in their prime and they *did* like their swim so much."

"A fox can't possibly have broken in. It must have been a person," remarked Marie.

"There's been a lot of fowl stolen round here lately. Old Tom Jackson lost two geese a couple of weeks back," Tibbles told them.

"Stolen for eating?" cried Lottie in horror.

"Oh, poor Flippy, poor Flappy!" wailed Charles.

"And they were always so good and layed so many eggs," moaned Jennet.

"They were always so happy and cheerful, never disgruntled or mouldy like hens," added Charles.

"It's awful to think that some fat person is eating them," said Lottie, "gnawing their poor little drum-sticks."

"Oh, shut up!" said Lucien, seeing Paul on the verge of tears again. "Who knows, somebody may be trying to play a practical joke on us and they may turn up after all."

But Lucien's optimism was of little avail, for ten minutes later Mrs. Butland—commonly known by the Pennyfields as *Butt*—arrived and confirmed all Tibbles' fears.

"That's what's 'appened," she said, "been pinched, like old Mother Todd's eggs and young Peel's Light Sussexes. They don't stop at nothing—them thieves. But that's the way of the world nowadays—stealing—even the young ones steal, brought up to it."

"We must get them back quickly, before they are killed," cried Jennet.

"*Killed,*" laughed the ancient Butt, taking off her steel-rimmed spectacles and rubbing them for no particular reason, "you needn't worry about that; they will 'ave wrung the poor things' necks before they ever got them out of the 'en-'ouse door. They don't want to cart a couple of live ducks around, don't you worry, to give the show away with their quacking."

At this reference to Flippy and Flappy's cheerful quacking, Paul left the room and sat on an apple tree in the orchard; and soon Dandylion meandered across and nibbled his toes; then Soloman came from the house and, jumping on the fallen trunk, sat beside him; for, although Soloman belonged to Lucien and Marie, he was a very affectionate dog and really more fond of Paul than was Paul's dog Brockie.

Meanwhile, in the dining-room the other Pennyfield children were discussing how the tragedy could best be remedied.

"I vote we go all out to catch the thieves," said Jennet.

"I think we should buy poor Paul some new ducks," suggested Lottie.

"No new ducks can ever be the same as Flippy and Flappy," said Marie.

"Time, the great healer," muttered Lucien.

"We've only got sixteen and sixpence left now," Sheila told them.

"We must make some more money. What about putting another advertisement in the Post Office—*Anything Done Anywhere By the Scholar Farm Useful Service*," sug- Lucien.

"That sounds a bit risky; supposing we are asked to swim the Channel or break in a notorious horse? What do we do then?" asked Marie.

"Well, haven't you any ideas? We've simply got to make an effort. It's not only that we want ponies and guns and canoes, but we must have a bit of odd money to pay for things when we break them. The other day, when Jennet had that big smash up and fell downstairs with a tray and broke four saucers, six cups, two egg-cups and one of the best glasses, poor Tibbles just didn't know what to do. She hasn't got all that amount of housekeeping money, you know, and she doesn't want to run up a lot of bills for Daddy on his return. I think she paid for the replacements out of her own wage on that occasion, which was awful."

"Oh dear," wailed Jennet, "but I couldn't help it; my foot just slipped."

"Don't whine," said Marie sharply. "No one suggested

you could have helped it. But Lucien's remarks have made it all the more obvious that we must earn some money. I know we get our weekly pocket lot to-morrow, but all added together, it only comes to two and sixpence and we always spend it on sweets and bus fares, so it might as well be counted as nil."

"Perhaps I had better not have my bee-hives, but, if we ate honey instead of jam, it *would* save Daddy some money," said Sheila.

"Well, anyway, Paul will have to wait for his ducks," said Marie.

"Let's think of a new and enticing advertisement, which will catch the eyes of all," suggested Lucien.

"I'm going to leave that to wiser brains than mine and do some bed-making," said Charles, hurrying from the room.

"I'm going to catch the thieves," Jennet told Marie, dashing into the garden.

"Don't forget to feed your cat," called Lucien.

"If she doesn't name that kitten soon, I'm going to. I want her in my circus," said Lottie, "and I'm going to rehearse now."

As Lottie left, the telephone bell rang and with a cry of "Hurray! perhaps it's a job in the offing," Marie ran into the hall and answered.

It *was* a job.

Mr. Phillips of Thrushfield Manor wanted ten windows cleaned inside and out, and he was delighted to hear that *The Scholar Farm Quick Window Cleaning Service* could do it this very morning.

"I shall be out," he said, "but my wife or the maid will be in; and could you tell your men to bring at least one good long ladder, because the attic window is rather high? And could you tell them also not to go prying around my buildings? Last time I had the window cleaners here they ate their sandwiches in my garage, poked around my toolshed and managed to let my wife's cat out, break a hamper and upset a can of petrol."

"Right, sir," replied Marie. "Your orders shall be carried out. Thank you. We will be round within an hour."

After recounting her conversation to Lucien and Sheila, she said, "Rather a peculiar man, I should think."

But Jennet, on hearing of his remarks about prying and of the squashed hamper, thought very differently. "Don't you see?" she shrieked. "He's the thief. It's as clear as night and day. Flippy and Flappy are probably sitting in the hamper waiting to be butchered. He probably doesn't realise that he stole them from *us*. Oh, Fate is kind! We must hurry or we will be too late."

And the twins' minds worked the same way. "Yes, quick!" they cried, tearing off to collect buckets.

"Oh, dear," said Marie, "I suppose we shall *have* to take them."

"They're going to be terribly naughty," warned Sheila.

"I'll make them behave," said Lucien. "And, whatever happens, Paul must come or he'll just sit and moulder and think about his ducks."

"I *do* wish Tibbles would give the twins a job," said Marie, fetching a bit of bread with which to catch Dandylion. "I *know* they will pry and I promised Mr. Phillips we would keep out of his sheds; they'll spoil everything."

"I don't know. I rather agree with Jennet. At least, I think there's a slight possibility that Flippy and Flappy were stolen by local people and I think we should leave no stone unturned in our search for them. Why should we not deny all connection with Jennet and the twins—that is, unless the ducks are found—and let them search the buildings?" suggested Lucien.

"They are sure to give the show away somehow," said Marie.

"I think it's a jolly good idea. They won't break any windows then," Sheila supported her brother.

Chapter Seven

THRUSHFIELD MANOR was grey, gabled and gloomy. Neglected ivy-clad trees stood in dismal silence round the ill-kept drive. The window frames and front door, once cream coloured, were chipped and dirty. The old white gate sagged on its hinges. The dark and dingy laurels smelt faintly of cats. As soon as the four older Pennyfields stepped within the garden, they were overcome by foreboding and despair. Lucien could see at a glance that their longest ladder was not long enough to reach the attic window. Marie felt sure that Mrs. Phillips would be furious when she found that *The Scholar Farm Quick Window Cleaning Service* was merely a pack of untidy and inefficient children. Sheila was certain that the twins and Jennet would be caught redhanded; they would be tried in a juvenile court, she decided, for attempted theft, and poor Daddy and Tibbles would be so upset. Paul knew suddenly that his ducks were dead; he could see them hanging up by their feet in a butcher's shop and harassed housewives hesitating over the price.

At the same moment the four Pennyfields stopped.

"This is awful," said Marie.

"I wonder where the twins are," said Sheila.

"Nothing venture, nothing win," quoted Marie, squaring her shoulders and pushing a dark lock of hair back into place.

"Oh for a beaker full of the warm south," quoted Lucien, shivering slightly.

"I think I shall tie Dandylion to that bush there," said Paul, pointing to a bedraggled flowering shrub, "but someone had better check my knot." He led the donkey across the narrow drive and the tailboard of the cart fell off and then all the buckets fell out with a loud clatter. As Lucien ran forward to help, a window opened with a dreary creak and a voice cried:

"What are you children doing in the garden? Go out at once."

A fair-haired woman in an overall looked down on them. She seemed to Paul very old—about fifty. Marie decided that she was the maid and said: "We've come to clean Mr. Phillips' windows. Where would you like us to tie our donkey?"

They looked rather odd—the four Pennyfields. Paul was wearing a pair of trousers which Lucien had passed down to him, and they were still too big, so he hitched them up with an enormous money belt; over these he wore his old

54

Thrushfield Manor was grey, gabled and gloomy.

coat with leather at the elbows. He had refused to come in his shorts, because, he said, they must all look as old as possible and he thought his coat was excellent, because he had seen hundreds of undergraduates, on his last visit to Oxford, wearing jackets patched with leather.

Sheila was tidily dressed—as always—but her dungarees, although spotless and neatly patched by her own hand, were too short and her legs gave the impression that they should not have appeared so soon. There was a little gap between the faded blue bottoms of her dungarees and her white ankle socks.

Of all the Pennyfields, Marie perhaps had the most dress sense; her clothes nearly always fitted well and she refused to allow Tibbles to buy her white ankle socks, combinations or long-sleeved woollen frocks; but she loved clear bright colours and clear bright colours looked very out of place in the garden of Thrushfield Manor. To-day she was wearing white tennis shoes, scarlet socks, a blue and white pleated skirt, a scarlet shirt—which her father had brought back from Brittany for Lucien very soon after the end of the war—and a pale yellow sleeveless pullover, which she promised to take off as soon as she had begun work. Lucien was wearing faded, red, fisherman's trousers, which had also come from Brittany, and a thick, brown, fisherman's jersey and canvas shoes with a hole in each toe.

The woman in the overall stared at them for a moment and then suddenly she burst out laughing.

"I don't know what my husband would say, I really don't. What a good thing he isn't at home. Oh, it is a good thing. It really is. *The Scholar Farm Quick Window Cleaning Service!* What a scream! And he's been telling all his friends about it—such a competent service—Major Dickens, Mrs. Barker, absolutely *everybody*—oh dear, what a scream. You are really it, aren't you? *The Scholar Farm Quick Window Cleaning Service*, I mean? You're not joking?"

"Yes, we are—for better or worse——" replied Lucien rather gruffly; he did not like being called a scream.

"I'm sure we can clean windows as well as any gang of men," said Marie, who possessed more self-confidence than any of her three companions.

56

"My dear, I'm *sure* you can. I wasn't laughing at you; just at the thought of my husband's remarks before he left this morning. I shouldn't tie your donkey there. I'll come down and show you a better place."

She disappeared.

"Silly woman," said Paul.

"Oh dear, I wonder what Jennet and the twins are up to. I hope they are not breaking anything. They *are* so clumsy. I expect they'll tear their clothes if they don't smash something," worried Sheila.

"If we tie both our ladders together, we still won't be able to reach that attic window," said Lucien, and, looking up to the top of the house, he felt suddenly small and weak, as though he would never have the strength to climb a ladder at all, let alone lift a bucket of water.

"Here she comes," said Sheila.

Mrs. Phillips appeared, wearing an old grey coat over her overall and showed them a useful post, where they could tie Dandylion.

"There we are," she said, that deed accomplished. "Now, we've got nothing really to worry about. I've shut my new Persian in the toolshed, so that you won't have to think about not letting him out and dear Smokey, she's my Persian she-cat, is all right anywhere, so there's no need to fuss about her either. I should start with the kitchen window first."

"Right-o," said Marie.

Cleaning the kitchen window was rather an embarrassing affair—or so Sheila thought. The maid, a small dark sceptical woman, was there and Sheila knew by the expression on her face that she thought the Pennyfields were a lot of silly kids.

She was in the process of making a vegetable stew and, as she wandered to and fro, she threw the poor window cleaners the most scornful glances. Lucien and Marie had started the passage windows, because they said it was foolish to leave the ladders standing idle, so it was Sheila and Paul whom the maid saw, and they did seem rather inefficient as they rubbed up and down and round and round on the dirty glass. Paul could not stop thinking of his ducks. Again he saw them hanging head downwards in a butcher's shop, only now the harassed housewives were replaced by jeering boys and the sawdust was stained with little drops of blood; and then this sordid scene was followed by another, set in a dining-room, where two greedy people—a fat man with a watch chain and a thick red face and a fatter woman with grey hair and false teeth—were eating at a small square table with a dirty white cloth and, of course, they were eating duck, picking at the drumsticks; and the woman's false teeth wobbled as she munched and her gums were very red, and she turned to her companion and said: "Very tough, aren't they, Bert? Whatever made you go and buy such old ones?" The longer Paul thought, the more he saw; and, because his mind was straying, he dropped his leather and then, without noticing that it had become dirty while on the ground, just picked it up and rubbed the window with it again. Of course this made great earthy smears and the maid saw and looked at Paul as though he was mad.

"Do take some trouble and attend," said Sheila, "and we'll never get finished before dark if you don't hurry up."

She was in difficulties, too. She had rubbed her pane with the soft yellow duster before the glass was dry and now it was covered in little bits of fluff. Every now and then she said, "Oh dear, oh dear!" as was her habit when anything went wrong.

Marie, perched precariously on a ladder, could hear her and, after a while, she could bear it no longer and called down, "Do stop whining."

Sheila was certain that the maid had heard Marie's rude remark; she fancied she saw her smile and felt very angry, so quietly, but with unusual vehemence for Sheila, she called back, "I wasn't whining. Don't be so jolly rude or I'll shake you off the ladder."

Marie, surprised and slightly alarmed by this unexpected threat, turned to look at her sister and, as she twisted herself on the ladder, her left foot slipped. For a moment she saw the rough cobbles below and thought that she was going to fall, fall and cut her head open; then, with a tremendous effort, she flung the bucket of water she was grasping into the air and grabbed a step above her with both hands; the ladder nearly overturned, nearly but not quite; it was the bucket which caused what Sheila considered to be a tragedy, and Paul was the victim. He had, at last, managed to forget Flippy and Flappy and was treating his four panes of window as a work of art. He had removed all the smears, remembered to see that they were dry before using the yellow duster and was just standing back to admire the result when the bucket came whizzing through the air, hit the corner of the back door porch and emptied most of its contents over Paul. As Lucien remarked afterwards, it was like a ridiculous act in a circus or variety show.

Sheila shrieked. The maid shrieked. Lucien cried, "You idiot." Marie shouted, "Look out." Only Paul was silent; he pushed his hand through his dripping dark brown hair and stared at the bucket.

"I'm terribly sorry," said Marie, and then she burst out laughing.

"It's not a bit funny," Sheila told her disapprovingly.

"Are you kids cleaning windows or are you playing the fool?" the maid asked, joining them in the garden.

Sheila went red with shame, right up to the roots of her hair. "Oh dear," she said, and realised that her panes were still fluffy.

"Definitely trying to clean windows," shouted Lucien from the top of his ladder, and Marie was glad that he was there; he was working on his third window and, with all his five foot ten, he looked reassuringly efficient.

"Well, I wish you could control your helpers or brothers and sisters or whatever they are," said the maid. "Look," she continued, seizing a duster from Sheila, "this is the way to do it." For about two minutes she rubbed vigorously and when she stopped the window was wonderfully clean and shiny. "There," she said, "that's the way to do it."

"Ah, an expert in our midst," said Lucien, winking at Sheila in an attempt to cheer her up.

"And what about this boy?" the maid went on, glancing at Paul, as though he was an object—a table or chair, thought Marie. "He's soaked; he had better come in and sit by the fire."

"Oh, thank you," cried Paul, who was heartily sick of

cleaning windows, "thank you very much indeed. Shall I take my shoes off; they are rather muddy?"

A moment later he was safely installed in the warm kitchen; his coat, looking shabbier than ever, his socks, which each had a large hole in the heel, and his duck's-egg green tie were hanging on a chair in front of the old-fashioned range and he was drinking a cup of tea and tasting a cheese savoury.

Presently Mrs. Phillips came in with a dustpan and brush. "Good gracious!" she said. "And what has happened now?"

The maid and Paul explained between them and Mrs. Phillips thought the whole affair was screamingly funny. Then she said that she knew of something that would warm him up; she had bought it for her son, because he seemed run down and was always catching colds. "It's the only tonic I can persuade him to drink," she said, leaving the kitchen and coming back again with a flagon of Australian burgundy.

"Oh, thank you," said Paul, "thank you very much." Then, a moment later, as he sipped the wine and felt it warm within himself, he said something that he had heard Lucien say: *"In vino veritas."*

"Hallo," said Mrs. Phillips, "do you know Latin already?"

"Oh yes, a little; I'm ten, you see, though actually Lucien taught me that; he knows lots of Latin, lots and lots; he's awfully good at languages. He knows some German and a little Italian and an awful lot of French." Paul, feeling rather grown up and very talkative, drained his glass, as though he had been drinking all his life.

Mrs. Phillips was silent for a moment, then she said: "Is Lucien the boy on the ladder? I wonder—oh, I don't know. How old is he? Or is it inquisitive to ask? Has he taken the school certificate?"

"He's sixteen, but not at all babyish for his age. He's been to France and Italy too and he knows an awful lot. He's going to pass the school certificate this summer. I expect he'll get an awful lot of credits." Paul felt that he must try to make up for all their earlier misdemeanours.

The maid seemed amused, but Mrs. Phillips remained

serious. After a pause she said, "Do you think he could come and have a word with me?"

That was how it started. As Marian remarked afterwards, *It's an ill wind that blows nobody any good*, and her bucketful of water was partly the cause of this unexpected piece of luck. Paul, of course, thought differently; he was of the opinion that it was his *little bit of diplomacy* that had won the day.

At the moment he showed none of the curiosity that he felt; but, leaping from his chair, cried, "Certainly, I'll fetch him," and ran out barefooted.

Lucien, hindered by a bucket, a tin of bluebell and a duster, was slow to descend the ladder and it was fully five minutes later when he heard the good news—that Mrs. Phillips would like him to coach her son Timothy in Latin and French, if her husband agreed. She would be willing to pay him quite a decent sum, if he worked well—say about two and sixpence an hour. "If you teach as well as you clean windows, I shall be more than pleased," she finished.

Chapter Eight

MEANWHILE, the twins and Jennet were beginning to enjoy themselves. Dressed in blue dungarees, yellow pullovers and scarlet, orange and green money belts, unaware that they were extremely conspicuous, they crept first into the garage and began investigating. After their weeding experience, Lottie and Charles were nervous. Twice they imagined that they heard footsteps and retreated behind a broken mower and two empty petrol tins to lie, covering themselves in grime, upon the old stone floor. Jennet called them cowards and talked in a noisy whisper, and searched without a qualm.

There was no car in the garage, but one obviously lived there some time during the day or night. There were several dirty, torn cardboard boxes, a brand new dustbin, a car battery, two spanners, two new tyres, a mass of empty gin, whisky and beer bottles and an old pram. Nothing, thought Lottie, to arouse suspicion; and then she moved a large box and changed her mind; for behind it was a pile of white feathers.

She let out a view-holloa, before remembering the need for quietness, and Lottie and Charles thought that somebody must be approaching and threw themselves on the floor and pulled an old tarpaulin over their heads. They looked so funny that Jennet began to giggle and then the twins thought that she had purposely yelled to frighten them and they were very cross. After a while, however, they rose to their feet again and looked at the feathers and became very excited.

"I knew it," whispered Jennet. "I knew there must be something fishy in the buildings as soon as Marie told me what Mr. Phillips had said. Fate is on our side, although I'm afraid Flippy and Flappy have been plucked by now."

"Poor ducks," said Charles, "poor, poor ducks. I would like to shoot the Phillipses."

"We must get some more proof; feathers are not enough. Perhaps, if we look around, we may find their yellow webbed feet. Sssh! Hide! Footsteps."

At Lottie's warning, the three of them flung themselves on the ground once more, and, this time, it was not a false alarm. Mrs. Phillips's maid walked by on her way to get some sticks, with which to light the boiler, and Charles's heart beat so fast that he thought it would burst and Lottie felt sure that the maid would hear her breathing.

The children lay quite still, covered by the tarpaulin, for a long time after the footsteps had died away.

"We mustn't be caught," whispered Lottie.

Then something happened which seemed to make their hearts stop beating. Somebody was pulling at the tarpaulin. I shall say we were playing hide and seek, thought Charles. Gosh! We are in for it, thought Lottie. I shall ask them what they've done with our ducks, decided Jennet. And then the pulling stopped and they heard a whine and suddenly it dawned on them that it was a dog. Cautiously Jennet crawled out, followed by the twins. The dog was Cockade and she jumped up at them with cries of delight. They all kissed and patted her and said that she should not have come, but none of them knew what to do with her.

Eventually they decided to tie her with Charles's big spotted handkerchief and Jennet's belt to one of the useful bushes.

"It's an awfully good thing she doesn't yell the place down, like Brockie," said Lottie, as they crept out and hid Cockade.

"Now," said Jennet, "we must investigate in here. Come on."

She opened the door of the toolshed and a grey-blue Persian cat ran out.

"Catch her, quick!" whispered Charles frantically.

But Jennet and Lottie seemed rooted to the spot; and then a terrible thing happened. Cockade, always so good with the cats at home, gave two wild yaps of excitement, tore Charles's handkerchief and raced after the Persian. Without thinking, Lottie followed them, while Jennet, attempting to stop Lottie, fell over a stray flint and broke her spectacles.

Each moment Lottie thought Cockade was going to grab and kill the cat, which did not have the sense to run up a tree, but made straight for the house. One behind the other, the three of them dashed down the garden path and, just as Mrs. Phillips was saying that she would pay Lucien two and sixpence an hour, they arrived at the back door.

"Gosh!" said Sheila.

"Lottie!" exclaimed Paul, forgetting that he must pretend she had nothing to do with him.

"'Ware, cat!" yelled Marie; "and dog—and child!"

"Tiddles, darling!" cried Mrs. Phillips.

"Cockade, Cockade," screeched Lottie.

Then the maid, who seemed the only one of the party who had kept her head, flung the back door wide, let the cat in and delivered Cockade a kick in the face.

"Oh don't, you beast! Don't kick her," cried Lottie.

"Oh dear, oh dear," said Sheila.

"What is happening? Take this West Highland away; it nearly killed Mrs. Phillips' show Persian, a very valuable cat." Lucien gave Lottie a meaning glance as he spoke.

"It's a catastrophe, and I'm terribly sorry. Cockade, you are a wicked and naughty dog," said Lottie, and, behind her back, she stuck a thumb up at Paul, so that he

63

could see that there was hope that the murderer of his ducks might yet be caught.

"Yes, she *is* a valuable cat and I don't know what stopped her from running out into the road and getting run over. She's only been here two or three days and hasn't got used to the place. She cost thirty guineas and I should never get another one like her. I would like to know how she got out, anyway."

Mrs. Phillips looked Lottie up and down, looked at her small, dirty, heart-shaped face, her tangled hair, her blue eyes—so like Lucien's.

"Is this child anything to do with you?" she asked, glancing in Marie's direction.

This is the end, thought Paul. All my tact has been wasted. Lucien's chances are ruined. I bet they haven't found Flippy and Flappy.

"I know her; but she's nothing to do with the window cleaning," Marie replied.

"To-day," added Sheila, who hated telling lies.

"Is the little cat all right or has she been nipped?" asked Lucien.

The maid spoke:

"Tiddles is all right, but what was the kid doing in the garden in the first place? And how did the cat get out of the workshop? That's what I should like to know. She's got some of your looks," the maid told Marie. "Is she your sister?"

At that moment Lucien pretended to trip over the bucket and with a loud clatter and a noisy grunt fell on the ground, almost at the maid's feet. "Sorry," he said, picking himself up slowly.

"Ow ooh! I've hurt my knee. Why on earth did I leave the bucket there. I'm so sorry, Mrs. Phillips. I haven't splashed you, have I?" He signalled frantically at Lottie to go while the coast was clear and Paul, who had thought that the maid had asked Marie whether the *cat* was her sister, started to giggle. Lucien threw Lottie a murderous glance and said:

"Well, back to the benches." Lottie took the hint, and shouting, "Good-bye, I'm terribly sorry," streaked off down the path with Cockade at her heels, to find Jennet crying because her spectacles were broken.

"Another expense," wailed Jennet. "All I do is cost money." She sniffed behind the bushes.

"Better have you *put to sleep*," said Charles cheerfully. "Sorry we didn't come to your rescue, Lot, but we thought you had plenty of helpers. What happened?"

"Don't call me *Lot*," said Lottie.

Chapter Nine

LUCIEN and Marie said that the feathers in the Thrushfield Manor's garage were of no importance, but the twins and Jennet thought differently. When they had tired of telling their elders that the feathers were an awfully good clue, they decided that they must take matters into their own hands.

The night after the tragic disappearance of Flippy and Flappy, Mr. Oldman, the owner of Thrushfield Farm, had lost ten of his best Rhode Island Reds and this made the three youngest Pennyfields all the more determined to catch the thief. They were unable to continue their investigations for two days, however, because on the day following their Thrushfield Manor search they had to go into Kingham with Tibbles to try on new clothes, and help Marie and Lucien clean the windows of a suburban villa on the outskirts of the little town of Tewkley. The day after this was Sunday, and as Tibbles was rather particular about Sunday, they had to go to church, wear respectable clothes and behave properly.

But on Monday they were determined to be idle no longer. They had planned to watch the Manor by night, to see Mr. Phillips return with a carload of stolen goods; and all the morning they felt very excited. Whenever Tibbles or Lucien asked them what they were plotting, they burst into giggles and eventually Sheila and Marie became annoyed by them and suggested that they might work and earn some money instead of spending all their time whispering and laughing.

C

Lucien spent the morning gardening and writing an article on The Virtues of Poverty, which he later decided was a smug, almost pious article, and tore up. Marie peeled all the vegetables for lunch, took the ferrets for a walk and tried to write a story called *A Pony for Two*. Sheila made an apple tart, helped Paul sew on a button and answered another advertisement for bee-hives—the last ones had turned out to be very expensive. Paul tried to do some mending, because Tibbles looked cross, and wrote a poem for the magazine, which started like this:

Sheila and Marie don't always agree,
    And one day they fought on a ladder.
They hurt not each other, but their ten year brother,
    And that makes the story sadder.

Their brother was me, just staring with glee
    At the temporary pride of my heart—
A window pane, with no single stain
    To make my pride depart.

Then, in a flash, there came a splash
    And my hair was dripping wet.
I said not a word, so no one heard
    Whether I was upset.

But I was not forsaken, and soon was taken
    Into a kitchen hot
And given wine, that was divine;
    And I drained the lot.

Charles and Lottie, stung by Marie's scornful words, also tried to write poetry. Without knowing it, they both attemped to write about their mice. They often had the same ideas—Charles and Lottie. Once they had dreamed the same dream. They supposed that it was because they were twins.

Charles only managed to write two lines:

Tick's never sick,
Though she eats awfully quick.

Lottie managed four:

> My mouse
> Has a house.
> Her name is Tock,
> But she hasn't a clock.

Marie said that both attempts were unworthy of the *Scholar Farm Magazine* and could not be published. Tibbles said why didn't the twins make their beds properly, instead of scribbling a lot of nonsense? But the twins did not mind these remarks. They only thought of the adventures in store for them. Lottie saw a rough, unshaven man in handcuffs being led to the police station by a grateful constable—for, of course, he had been captured by the three youngest Pennyfields, who, risking their lives, had chased him for hours across treacherous country in the terrible, pitch-black darkness of a wild and stormy night. Charles thought of his triumphant return in the early morning with a duck under each arm, of Paul's delight and Tibbles' incredulous praise, and Jennet, who had spent a large part of the morning trying to write a song for her variety show, because she was under the impression that she would be taken up for libel if Sheila sang a song composed by any one out of the family, saw—when she thought about their coming excursion—the headlines of a paper, which said: *Three children aged eight and nine catch well-known poultry thief after daring and courageous chase.* Of course there was a photograph, too, and Jennet had remembered to take off her spectacles, for once, and so looked better than usual.

And then at last the long day ended. Evening came and twilight and the guinea fowl went to roost in the old Blenheim tree; and the moon rose behind the granary and lit the little orchard with silver. Lottie and Jennet could not sleep, but lay staring at the wallpaper, which was pale blue with red birds flying like swallows across to yellow leaves, and at the four pictures—a drawing of a wire-haired terrier, which Sheila had bought for one and sixpence; a hunting scene in water colour; a sunny picture of cherry trees in blossom and a little painting of St. Francis feeding the birds—and at the numerous postcards, which they had fixed on the walls with drawing-pins, and at the numerous ornaments on the Georgian chimneypiece.

"Sheila will soon be coming to bed. We must pretend to be asleep. I don't know how we are to get out without waking her." Lottie giggled as she spoke. Now that they had definitely decided to watch Thrushfield Manor, the thought of the daring deceitfulness needed to carry out their proposition appalled her. Never before had they ventured out alone at night. Tibbles would be absolutely livid if she caught them and Lottie felt that she would not be able to blame her for her anger. It seemed a gigantic task that they had set themselves and she was frightened by her own daring.

"It will be jolly difficult to waken Charles," Jennet replied after a pause. Then they both began to giggle again.

Next door Charles was fast asleep. He shared a room with Paul and he knew that Paul would waken him when he came to bed. He would want to play the torch game. It was a simple and exciting form of amusement and they had never been caught. They each had a torch and one was *he* and chased the other one's light across the ceiling, along the walls, twisting in and out of the pictures. Their room had been redecorated lately; it had been Paul's idea and Lucien had helped him. The walls were primrose yellow and the door and window frame pale green—like daffodils, Paul had said. But his father and Tibbles did not like the colour scheme. Mr. Pennyfield did not like the woodwork and the nurse thought beige and dark brown would have been a more suitable combination, especially for a boy's room. Charles did not really mind what the room looked like. He was rarely in it, except when going to bed, changing or dressing; and he always fell asleep at once and never wakened early like Paul, to think of poetry and ducks and see the sun rising.

Jennet found it very difficult indeed to waken him at a quarter past ten that night. It was raining outside; she could hear the water gurgling in the gutters; and she had lost her spectacles. Charles's obstinacy, she told herself, was the last straw. She turned away and was thinking of

68

her warm bed when he opened his eyes, grunted and sat up.

"Oh, yes—the feathers and the car—we are going out to-night, aren't we? Have Tibbles and Lucien gone to bed?" He swung his legs out and stood shivering on the rush mat as he spoke.

"They went early—half an hour ago—but you had better be quiet, because they're probably not asleep yet. Have you seen my spectacles?"

At half-past ten the three of them were walking in silence down the lane. All of them wished that they had stayed in bed, but not one was going to admit it. The rain had turned out to be only an April shower and the sky was clear now, except for a few skittish clouds which endeavoured to hide the moon whenever the children reached a lonely spot. After a while Jennet said:

"Let's sing. It might make things more cheerful."

But the twins thought her suggestion was foolish. A lot of noise would warn Mr. Phillips of their approach. So they walked on in silence, regretting their venture more and more with each stride. On the road they met several parties of people returning from the Red Hart and a few bicyclists. One man called out and asked if they were running away from home and after that they took care to move into shadow when they heard or saw any one coming.

At length they reached Thrushfield Manor and felt a pleasant sensation of triumph. Now there was no turning back. But the sense of triumph soon faded. As they crept up the back drive, Lottie was worried by another thought. . . . It might be clever to creep up here in the dark without any one knowing, but wasn't it mean to watch the house of one who was about to employ their brother? Yesterday Lucien had been interviewed by Mr. Phillips, had read Latin and written Latin and met with approval. To-morrow he was to start coaching Timothy and would earn five shillings and be paid by the very man whose downfall they were now plotting. That was how it seemed to Lottie. It goes against the grain, she thought—it was a phrase that Marie often used. But then what could one do?

69

There were poor Flippy and Flappy to consider. Their death *must* be revenged. It was worth risking Tibbles' anger, worth being mean if they caught the murderer.

She consoled herself with this thought as they peered into the garage. The double doors were locked; but Charles had not forgotten his electric torch and he shone it through the window.

"The car's there and there are some hampers piled up close by with a rug half over them." His voice was an octave higher than usual and the others, too, were excited by this news. They each borrowed his torch in turn and peered through the window. Then they retreated to hide in the bushes and await further developments.

"Gosh! Supposing we do catch them. Won't it be funny? Paul will be pleased. Won't every one be surprised, though? They'll all say you have the second sight, Jennet," Lottie said, sitting down on the damp ground.

"Somehow, I knew from the first, as soon as Marie told me about keeping out of the buildings. It's Fate. It's Fate."

If Lucien or Marie had been present at that moment they would have told Jennet to stop being melodramatic, because they did not want her to grow up into the sort of person who imagines she sees visions or describes herself as psychic. But, as they were not there, she continued to dramatise the situation, until the twins began to feel that theirs was indeed a noble venture. The fact that the police, who had been told of the disappearance of the ducks two days ago, had done nothing to discover the thief, made them feel that their coming triumph was all the greater.

Soon, crouching or sitting behind the bushes, they became cold and stiff and decided to take it in turn to walk round the back of the buildings. But it was eerie by one-self, especially after one o'clock when a blanket of dark clouds rolled up from the west and covered their friend the moon.

Lottie began to fuss about Charles. He had had bronchitis last winter and it suddenly dawned on her that sitting in the damp to-night might start another bout.

"Tibbles would be furious," she said, and, "Supposing you died. It would be an awful catastrophe. What on earth

70

would we do? If nothing happens soon, we'll have to go home and I don't care what you think, Jennet."

And then, at half-past five, something began to happen. A man, who they guessed was Mr. Phillips, walked down the garden path from the back door, unlocked the garage and put the hampers in the car.

The three children could hardly keep still with excitement. They had always thought that only people in books caught thieves. Charles was suddenly afraid that they would not succeed; it seemed ridiculous that Jennet, Lottie and himself should be clever enough to be at the right place at the right moment. And then he realised how helpless they really were, how easily Mr. Phillips could knock them on the head and dispose of their bodies. They were not ready for violence; they had brought no weapons, he reflected, and with this reflection came an awful empty feeling in the pit of his stomach. His hands were cold and sticky as he watched Mr. Phillips leave the garage and walk away towards the house.

"He's left the door unlocked," whispered Jennet. "Now to see what's in the car. I bet it's ducks. Now or never! Victory or death!" Her hands were sticky, too, and when she jumped to her feet, her knees felt wobbly; they almost knocked together.

"Jennet! Stop! We must arm ourselves first. There are some sticks round the back," cried Charles, and he ran behind the buildings, followed by Lottie.

Jennet had not heard all he had said—just the cry of *stop*. When she turned to see what had happened, the twins had disappeared. She peered round the back, but, without her spectacles, she could not see them; then she thought that they might have slipped past her in the darkness and might now be in the garage. She ran through the double doors and opened the car door; the hampers were on the seat and there was something alive and rustling inside them. Could it be ducks? She paused and wished the twins were here, and then she saw something that terrified her— a torch coming down the path from the house.

There was no escape now; it had almost reached the garage door. If she tried to run out she would be caught. She never thought of hiding behind the mower. At that

71

moment there seemed only one escape—the car. Without hesitation she leapt in, shut the door and covered herself with the rug. She was just in time. A few seconds later the torch shone bright in the garage.

And then the man who they thought was Mr. Phillips was getting into the car and turning on the headlights; and presently they left the garage, drove down the drive and out into the road.

All the feeling of excitement and importance left Jennet. She felt a knot rising in her throat; she wanted to sniff; she was sure Mr. Phillips would hear her breathing in a moment and she was nearly overcome by a terrible feeling of sickness and dread. She pinched herself in the hope that it might all be a dream and she might waken to find herself in bed, to see the blue wallpaper and the dear red birds and the familiar postcards. Never before had she wished so much for the comfort and security of her bedroom; but she did not waken; the dark musty rug still covered her; the smell of fowl and feather was still strong. The car jolted and jerked and then, down in her toes, she felt the first signs of pins and needles. . . .

Chapter Ten

WHEN the twins realised that they had lost Jennet they were terrified. They searched the garage and all the bushes again and again.

"Tibbles *will* be cross," wailed Lottie.

"Supposing she's been hit over the head," moaned Charles.

They made these two miserable remarks at least a dozen times in ten minutes and then a new and horrible thought struck them. Supposing there was a well hidden somewhere in the garage or the bushes and she had been pushed or had fallen into it? Now they searched again with renewed ardour, groping in the darkness, feeling on the ground for the lid of a well.

"He might have chucked her in and slammed the top," Charles suggested.

"Oh, how I wish we had never come to this beastly place!" cried Lottie.

Every time they glanced at the house they were overcome by gloominess. Now, with the first grey streaks of dawn lighting the eastern sky, the ugly gables, the shabby cracked window frames, the strong front door, the ivy-clad trees—so still on this windless April morning—all seemed to the twins to tell the same terrible story.

This was the sort of place where murders were committed, where innocent, unsuspicious people, men, women and young children, met their death. Who could tell how many traps and wells were hidden for this purpose? The twins did not read much, but they had not left the ghastly thrillers, the spy stories and the detective books of Lucien's early youth untouched. They did not listen to the wireless often, but Tibbles never failed to hear the creepier serials, the more breath-taking plays and sometimes they would see her listening with a rapt expression, gripping her chair with both hands and then they would listen, too; until they had really begun to believe that the murdering of people was quite an everyday occurrence, practised by some criminals more as a sport than anything else.

They felt the walls for trap-doors and Charles climbed on to the rafters in the garage and all the time they called, quite quietly, "Jennet, where are you? Jennet, where are you?"

Then, as day came and the cocks stopped crowing, they turned for home, miserable, cold and hungry.

"If only she had had her spectacles, she might not have been caught so easily," said Charles.

"What will the others say? Supposing she really is dead? And it will all be our fault for running round the back to get sticks. We might have heard her cries if we hadn't been so busy looking for weapons. Oh dear, Tibbles will be furious! And what will poor Cockade say?"

At the thought of Jennet struggling alone in a well and the West Highland terrier's misery, Lottie began to cry.

"What will Daddy say? That's more to the point," Charles told her. "Poor, poor Jennet, but perhaps she's not dead at all; perhaps she fell through a door into a secret passage and is, at this moment, saving the lives of hundreds of ducks. Perhaps she'll get her photograph in the paper like she wanted or perhaps she'll be given a huge reward—ten pounds or something—or a medal from the R.S.P.C.A., or perhaps her name will become a household word."

"Perhaps she got into the car," shrieked Lottie suddenly, "and is tracing the thieves to their lair. While we have been searching, she has been listening to their conversation. Oh, won't she have a lot to tell the police!"

"Yes, that's what happened. Why didn't we think of it before. What a clever idea. She must be excited—a real spy. I *wish* I had seen her and got in too."

It was with this cheerful conclusion uppermost in their minds that the twins reached Scholar Farm and rushing into the dining-room, yelled, "Jennet's catching the thieves. She's in their car now." They were met by silence, complete and absolute. Even the clock seemed to have stopped ticking and the dining-room was empty, empty even of dogs. The twins looked at each other helplessly. They had both jumped to the same terrible conclusion—Jennet was dead, that was clear now; the police had rung up and the rest of the family and Tibbles had gone to identify the corpse, and the dogs, unnoticed, had followed.

Lottie found her voice first. "Oh, why did we ever go?" she asked. "I wish I was dead," said Charles. They walked into the kitchen, which seemed strangely cold, because the range, usually lazing gaily at this hour, had not yet been lit; grey unfriendly ashes lay in the grate and brought Death and the Devil to Lottie's mind; for, often, she had chanted in happier moments: *Ashes to ashes, dust to dust; if God won't have you the devil must.*

And she also knew *Horatius: The ashes of his fathers and the temples of his gods. . . .*

Ashes—ashes—Jennet's ashes, thought Lottie, and she felt so sick that she had to sit down on a chair by the range; it was while she was sitting on the chair that she saw the notice that Lucien had hung on the dresser for her to read. She leapt to her feet, called to Charles and pulled it from the hook.

She read:
Jennet, Lottie, Charles—Look!

74

If you return here, do not search for us. We are search-
ing for you. Light the boiler if you like and make some
toast for Tibbles. We will be back about nine. . . . Lucien.

"They haven't heard that Jennet is dead. They think
she's with us. Hurray!" said Lottie. "She's probably all
right, then."

"We are in for the most terrible row—bed for the rest
of the day I should think," said Charles. "I wonder if she
is in that car; she may have heard an awful lot, saved lots
and lots of ducks."

"*We* shan't get in such a row, then. Come on, let's try
to light Blazing Bill."

Their hopes rising every moment, the twins started to
rake out the ashes. . . .

While the twins were searching frantically amongst the
bushes around the garage at Thrushfield Manor, Jennet
was gingerly peering from underneath the decrepit old
rug. She was disappointed now, sadly disappointed.

Her first feelings of terror having disappeared, she had
soon begun to hope that Mr. Phillips might pick up another man, an accomplice, so that she would learn their
plans or at least know where they were going. But now,
after what seemed an age, Mr. Philllips was still alone and
Mr. Phillips by himself was a very dull person; he whistled
occasionally and hummed in an extremely annoying manner, but he gave no clue to his character; he didn't even
mutter or curse or talk to himself like Butt. So Jennet had
decided to have a peep round. If she had not forgotten her
spectacles, or rather, lost them, things might have been
easier, but still, she reflected, *it was no use crying over*
spilt milk; she must do what she could without them.

The pins and needles had reached her knees and her
neck felt stiff. Slowly, cautiously, she crawled from underneath the rug and, twisting her head round, peered on to
the seat. The hampers were there; they had wide slits in
the lids and, now that it was light, she could see the pris-
oners crouching within. They were not white, as she had
thought before, but grey; and they were not ducks, nor
even hens, nor show bantams; they were pigeons with
rings on their legs—homing pigeons.

She heard Mr. Phillips moving in the front of the car

and hastily lay on the floor again and pulled the rug over herself, realising with disgust that these pigeons were probably not stolen at all, but merely entering for a race this morning.

For some time now, Jennet stayed very still trying to decide which was her best line of action. She was not the sort of person to suffer unneceassry discomfort and, if Mr. Phillips was no thief, but a perfectly respectable man taking his pigeons to compete in some perfectly respectable race it was obviously unnecessary for her to remain hidden; she must think of an excuse for her odd behaviour, that was all. Presently, as they passed through a little grey stone village, she had an idea and, with the pins and needles creeping up her legs once more, a feeling of stiffness in her neck and shoulders, she decided to try it out straight away. Clearing her throat with a little cough, she spoke and, after so much silence her voice sounded unfamiliar and shrill.

"I say," she said. "What time do you have to be there?"

Mr. Phillips braked, throwing her against the front seat as the car jerked to a standstill. Then he turned round and looked at her, and suddenly Jennet felt confused, her face grew hot. "What are you doing here?" he asked.

"I hope you don't mind. I know it's unusual to find stowaways in cars; but I do want to see pigeons race—I've always wanted to. And when I saw you setting off to-day the temptation—well, I couldn't help getting in. You don't mind frightfully, do you? I'm awfully sorry. What lovely pigeons. Have they got names?"

She spoke loudly and clearly, but her hands were shaking.

"*Well*, of all the cheek!" exclaimed Mr. Phillips, staring at her incredulously. "Thought you would just hop in when my back was turned, did you?"

He looked amazed by her words, amazed, but not cross. He was about forty-five and his face was haggard; there was nothing strong or obstinate about his features; she was surprised that his wife should have seemed frightened of him. Jennet's hands stopped shaking and she grinned.

"It was the best way of getting there, after all," she said "I think you have to be a bit original, if you want to get

Jennet crawled from underneath the rug.

on and do things and be famous, don't you? Lucien says you have to."

'Lucien, Lucien? Not the Pennyfield boy who's going to coach Timothy?"

Too late, Jennet realised her mistake. The others would be furious, of course, but she wasn't going to tell any more lies if she could avoid it. After all, they couldn't judge Lucien by her behaviour, she decided. She would tell the truth.

"He's my brother and he's awfully good at coaching and that sort of thing. He's awfully good at *everything* really. He would be furious if he knew where I was now. Do you think I might watch the pigeons start off, please?" She wanted to get off the subject of Lucien as soon as possible.

"It wouldn't hurt Timothy to develop a bit more spunk anyway," said Mr. Phillips, "although I don't want him hopping into strangers' cars—it's a dangerous occupation, you know. By the way, what about your parents? Are they aware of your——? No, I suppose not. If it was Timothy I should be worried to death."

The thought of the people at Scholar Farm worrying about her had not entered Jennet's head. Now she realised that they might have found her bed empty, if the twins had not yet returned, and would be in a terrible fuss.

"Oh gosh!" she said. "Are you very late? Have you got much farther to take the pigeons? If it's not an awful bother, do you think I could possibly get out farther on and ring up Tibbles or Lucien and explain? Only I've forgotten to bring any money. Could you possibly lend me tuppence? Lucien can pay you back to-morrow. I'm terribly sorry."

"You don't mean get out and try to make your own way home, do you? Because I'm not having that. You'll jolly well have to stick it out now and see the pigeons start and I can tell you, it's not very thrilling for those not genuinely interested. We've got quite a long way to go yet, too. That's why I started so early; but I'll certainly lend you enough money to ring up your parents. If I remember rightly, there is a kiosk a little farther on. You're very lucky to be let off so easily; you deserve to be severely punished. How old are you—ten? eleven?"

"I haven't got any parents, at least not to be worried. Daddy's abroad somewhere. Tibbles, she's our nurse, bets it's Russia. Actually I'm nine, but I'll soon be ten. Look! Whoa, please! There's the telephone."

As Mr. Phillips felt in his pockets for some pennies, Jennet wished that she had not spent the half-crown given to her for such emergencies as these—although, of course, she would never regret buying the bedraggled kitten, now named Spookie, because of her strange witch-like expression.

"I say, thanks awfully," said Jennet. "But these enclosed telephones are awfully difficult. Do I just put the money in, press a button and speak? Our number's Thrushfield 100."

"I'll put you through," said Mr. Phillips, with a sigh. "But we had better hurry up or I shall be late. Come on, move out of the way."

"Sorry," said Jennet.

It was five past nine. Tibbles and the four eldest Pennyfields had just returned and, when the telephone bell rang, the house was in an uproar.

Lucien was lecturing Charles quietly but very ferociously. Marie was shaking Lottie and telling her that she *must* have seen Jennet disappear.

Tibbles was shouting: "Someone had better go and ring up the police and tell them we've got two. I've made a proper fool of myself. What your poor father would say if he was here, I *don't* know, that I don't. And now where's Jennet? Acting the fool somewhere, I suppose. It would serve you all right if I caught my death of cold and you 'ad to darn your own socks and cook your own meals, that it would. After all I've done for you, you go and treat me like this. . . ."

Marie thought that she had never been so glad to hear the telephone in all her life, as she was at that moment; but, when she picked up the receiver, she was stricken with terror; her knees really did knock against each other. She had hoped, almost expected, to hear Jennet's voice.

Mr. Phillips' rather dreary, "Is that Thrushfield one hundred?" seemed to spell disaster. The next sentence would surely say that a little girl with fair hair had been found dead in a ditch or fatally injured in a motor accident? This is the end, thought Marie, gripping the table with one hand. But, of course, she was wrong; for, as soon as she had managed a miserable *yes*, Jennet spoke and there was no doubt that Marie had never before and has never since been so pleased to hear her sister Jennet's voice.

"Hallo, it's Marie—isn't it? I say, they weren't duck thieves. I mean he wasn't (I can't talk too loud, because *he's* just outside). And I'm going to watch some pigeons start off or something; it's going to be awful fun. I do hope you weren't awfully worried. And that Lottie and Charles explained about me being trapped in the car—wasn't it awful? All because I forgot where I had put my spectacles, really. I say, I hope the twins got back before you woke up and found we had gone. I shall have to stop in a minute, because Mr. Phillips is outside and he's in a hurry. He's been awfully decent, but I've had to tell masses of lies—whoppers. I couldn't say we thought he was a thief." Jennet paused.

"You're a beast," said Marie, "an absolute beast. Poor Tibbles has nearly gone off her head with worry. And how do you think you're going to get back from where you are and who do you think is going to pay for your lunch? Mr. Phillips, I suppose. Everybody has been searching for you —Mr. Bennet, the police, Mrs. Smudge, even the postman's been looking. I suppose you think it's clever to stay out all night. . . ."

"Hoi, give the telephone to me," interrupted Lucien. He didn't reproach Jennet; he thought she would get enough of that later, but he found out what time she would be back and then spoke to Mr. Phillips and said how very sorry he was that she had been such a nuisance. He was a little mystified when Mr. Phillips said that anyway he was glad to think that he would be satisfying what, apparently, had been a life's desire—Jennet's longing to see the pigeons starting on their long journey homewards. But Lucien did not ask questions; he merely laughed politely and then they rang off.

They were all relieved to hear of Jennet's safety, but relief did not lessen Tibbles' anger. After a hurried meal of porridge, toast, margarine and marmalade, the twins were sent to bed for the rest of the day. Paul was told to take off his jacket, wash his face and hands again, brush his hair and try to look respectable. Sheila was told to stop talking in "that silly, whiney way." Marie was sent to buy rhubarb and Lucien to ring up the police.

When the four eldest Pennyfields had accomplished these tasks, made their beds and washed up the breakfast things, they hurried to the granary and held a council of war. Lucien had called it and, sitting on the wobbly, home-made steps, he pointed out that during the last week they had earned little money—very little, when you considered the price of ponies, guns and canoes. He said that they had neglected their gardens, not even thought about the suggested puppets and only sent in the most feeble contributions for the magazine. They had also been slow and extremely inefficient window cleaners, which was the reason for them not being employed more often.

Marie, Sheila and Paul agreed with Lucien and then Sheila produced a letter which had come by post that morning and, to her surprise, was an answer to her advertisement. A Miss Frankie White wanted to know how much she would charge for typing a three-hundred page novel. It was written in a sprawling looped hand and ended: "In anticipation of an early reply, Yrs faithfully, Frankie White (Miss)."

"A very queer letter," remarked Paul.

"What terrible pink writing paper," said Marie.

After they had all inspected the letter several times and drafted a reply, in which they said the charge would be four pounds, they returned to the first subject—the earning of money. Lucien wanted the ferrets to work more; he thought it was ridiculous for two animals, which were sick of their hutches, to sit in them, day after day, eating food and earning nothing; so Lucien and Marie drafted an advertisement to be put in the post offices: *The Scholar Farm Ratters. These excellent and ferocious ferrets will kill your rats quickly and efficiently. Safer than poison. Easier*

D

than guns. Charge, 3/- per rat killed. Tel. Thrushfield 100.

This deed done, Lucien left for Thrushfield Manor and Timothy's company. Sheila and Marie started work in their gardens. Paul exercised the tortoises and the mice and then took Janet and Judas for a walk on collars and leads. He thought it was important that they should behave well the first time they were employed.

Meanwhile, Jennet was driving homewards, trying to forget that Tibbles would be very cross with her when she returned, trying to forget that she had spent two shillings on a fruitless and foolish errand—for she was determined that Mr. Phillips should be paid back the money he had spent on her telephone call and on the snack they had eaten in a roadside café. . . .

Chapter Eleven

THE very next day their hopes rose and Marie, who answered the telephone, drove a hard bargain. Paul and Charles were particularly delighted; it was just the sort of job they liked—a cocktail party and they were to be the waiters; at least some of the Pennyfields were; Marie was not sure that the twins were wanted. But what raised their hopes was the money. Marie had just heard of a 14.2 pony for sale for fifty pounds and she was feeling frustrated and so she had said that the charge would be a pound for the evening and the affected voice at the other end of the telephone had said that that would be quite all right.

"Of course it's not for two days; but a *pound*—that's an awful lot. I do hope you didn't sound mercenary or grabbing: I hope it isn't too much to ask," said Paul.

"It's jolly little," answered Marie, "and she sounded jolly relieved, I can tell you."

Most of the Pennyfields worked in their gardens during the morning and, thinking of the cocktail party, whistled and sang while they worked. But there was one blot—Lottie; she was in bed with a temperature, the result, Tibbles said, of spending a night out. Jennet was particularly upset; secretly, she felt that it was her fault, and Tibbles did not make her conscience any easier. She made

82

Jennet spend the whole day indoors, helping with the housework.

Then, at lunch, a terrible thing happened. Tibbles said that *none* of them were to go to the cocktail party.

"I'm sick to death of all this gallivanting around and if you think I'm going to have any more of you in bed, you're mistaken," she finished.

Her announcement was met by dead silence. Marie gave Jennet and Charles a hard reproachful glance which said, all too plainly, *your fault*. Lucien stopped eating and put his hands in his pockets. Then, suddenly, Charles burst into tears and Sheila said, "Oh dear," and Marie said, "Don't be silly, Charles," and Lucien said, "We won't catch cold there; it's as warm as toast."

"What are you crying for, Charles?" asked Tibbles, and, as Charles seemed unable to make a reply, Marie said:

"Because he wanted to go to the party and earn a pound."

"Well, *he's* not going whatever 'appens. I can tell you that straight. I suppose if Lucien wants to go I can't stop him."

"What about me?" asked Marie, but Lucien prodded her under the table. Then Charles found his voice:

"It's all my fault," he wailed, "and I did want to go so much, so very much."

At his words, Jennet started to cry too. "It isn't your fault, it's mine," she said.

"I should think it *is* about time that you felt sorry, with poor Lottie in bed and all," scolded Tibbles.

"Have some more rhubarb tart, Charles," suggested Lucien.

"Honestly, Tibbles, we won't catch cold," said Paul, "and think, if we don't learn to work while we are young, we'll grow into awful lazy grown-ups." Lucien prodded him too late. Tibbles had already seized upon the remark.

"I'll tell you what," she said. "If you want to learn to work, you try to make your bed a bit better and keep your clothes a bit tidier and be a little more civil when I ask you to run along to the grocer's, and write to your father more often. You can improve yourselves at 'ome all right, without gallivanting off to wait and wash up in strangers' houses."

"Nobody said anything about washing up and we are really going because we want to earn a pound, whatever Paul likes to say," replied Marie hotly.

"Ssssh," said Lucien.

"If you can't stop crying, you'd better go upstairs to your rooms," said Tibbles, and Jennet and Charles left the table.

Then, using all the tact he could muster, Lucien started to talk round Tibbles; he said that they would be helping out someone, who was in a terrible fix with no servants, that it would be good experience for them, because (a) they would learn how to behave at cocktail parties—after all, it wouldn't be very long before they were old enough to start going to them; (b) they would learn how to *run* cocktail parties, so that if either Marie or himself married, they would make a good host or hostess and not behave like a bewildered hobbledehoy; (c) they would see the beautifully arranged trays, the elegant cut glass and shining silver, the decorative flowers and the speckless carpets and all this brilliance, this perfect orderliness, this dazzling loveliness could only affect them in one way—they would become more conscientious at home; they would realise that they were untidy and lazy and they would bring in and arrange flowers, and clean the silver, and keep the dogs off the chairs; and wipe their feet more often, so that the carpets would be cleaner; and generally behave in a more helpful and civilised manner.

Tibbles said, "Oh yes, I've 'eard that one before."

But Lucien and Marie saw the change in her countenance and knew that she was *coming round*—as Butt would put it.

By the time the washing up was done, they had gained permission for themselves and Sheila to go to the cocktail party. Paul was bitterly disappointed. But, upstairs, Jennet and Charles were feeling more cheerful. They had dressed up as cavaliers and were rehearsing for the variety show and Lottie was shouting advice from her bed.

In the end Paul *did* go to the cocktail party. Sheila caught Lottie's chill? 'flu?—nobody seemed able to say

84

what it was exactly—and was forced to spend the day in bed. Now, clothes presented a difficulty. It had been all right before, because Sheila possessed several very respectable frocks, but Paul's grey flannel shorts and best jacket were far from smart. Lucien and Marie tried to iron them, but without success; he had not folded or hung them properly and they were horribly creased and crumpled, and the jacket had paint on the elbows. They did not dare to ask Tibbles to help them, because their venture was still far from popular. Then suddenly Marie had what she described as a brainwave.

"I've got it," she yelled.

"Not the 'flu?" asked Paul.

"No, an idea—Lucien's old fancy dress—you can wear it."

"What, go as a pirate?"

"Yes, Mrs. Smith-Thomas will probably think it an *absolute scream*."

"She's not Mrs. Phillips."

"I didn't say she was."

"There's no reason to think that she talks like Mrs. Phillips."

"All right then, she'll think it's *perfectly divine*. I spoke to her on the telephone. I know what she's like. Don't you think the fancy dress is a jolly good idea, Lucien?"

"I think it's the only way out. It'll look a bit funny, only one of us dressed as a pirate. It would be better if we could *all* wear fancy dress, but that's impossible. You had better try it on, if you still want to come, Paul."

The bell-bottom trousers proved to be too long, but Marie said she would take them up and the scarlet shirt, the buckled shoes, the enormous belt, the spotted kerchief and the brass buttoned jacket all fitted beautifully.

"There's one advantage," said Lucien, "you needn't bother to wash your face. Pirates are awfully dirty people."

"If he's too filthy, the guests won't fancy their food," Sheila called down from her bed.

"I quite agree," said Marie, "a few careful bloodstains on the cheek will be suitable and picturesque or a scrape or two with charcoal, but not ordinary dirt and you *must* wash your hands."

85

It was five o'clock when they eventually set off down the lane. Paul felt rather self-conscious in his pirate costume, but Lucien and Marie chattered gaily enough.

Mrs. Smith-Thomas, who greeted them, was small, fortyish, with very blonde hair (Marie and Lucien had an argument afterwards over whether it was bleached or natural), very pale blue eyes, blackened lashes, a greasy skin and thin lips. She was heavily made up with long pointed, varnished finger-nails and she wore a pale blue frock, which Paul said was unsuitable for a woman of her age. She was a little surprised to find that *The Scholar Farm Useful Service* employed children to do their work, but Lucien explained that one of the best waitresses was sick in bed and that Paul was useful and accustomed to carrying trays (this was partly true, because, during the last three days, he had taken up most of Lottie's meals). Mrs. Smith-Thomas said she hoped the other waitress would soon recover and that Paul looked very sweet. Then Captain Smith-Thomas appeared and she explained about the sick waitress to him and he told Paul to wash the bloodstains from his face.

"But I couldn't do that, sir," said Paul; "it's all part of the get-up and I had to prick my finger very hard to get enough blood and Jennet singed her hair making charcoal for the black marks."

"Oh I *see*," said Captain Smith-Thomas in patronising accents. "In that case it is quite *impossible* for you to do anything about it."

Mrs. Smith-Thomas showed them the trays; there were four silver ones laden with delicious morsels of food and three very large mahogany ones with countless glasses of sherry and cocktails on them.

"When you have emptied them of food or drink go to the hatch in the dining-room—here, I will show you—and Elsie will have a whole row of glasses and more plates of eats waiting on this shelf, see?" Mrs. Smith-Thomas explained. "But, anyway, talk it over with Elsie."

She left them looking through the hatch at a fat, friendly cook.

"Well, are you these marvellous waiters?" asked the cook, with a grin.

"Not marvellous—willing, that's all. Are they expecting many people?" asked Marie.

"About forty. I don't know why they didn't do anything about getting extra waiters before; daft, I call it— leaving everything so late. Of course, they didn't know that Pam was going to give in 'er notice when they sent the cards out, nor that Doris was going to catch the 'flu; but still them two girls wouldn't be enough. What are you —a pirate?" She looked at Paul.

"Supposed to be," he muttered.

Nobody arrived until six-thirty, when a very fat man and a very dark woman appeared on the scene and, after exclaiming, "My dear, *don't* say we are the first?" ventured into the drawing-room and, seeing Paul, cried, "But what an absolutely *sweet* little boy." Paul disappeared into the dining-room abruptly and Lucien and Marie offered them sherry or cocktails and a delicious assortment of food.

A few moments later several carloads of guests arrived and, from then onwards, the Pennyfields were kept busy. Lucien and Marie were excellent waiters, but Paul was inattentive and absent-minded. Once he actually offered a tall young business man an empty tray, saying, "Won't you have something—a lobster patty?—they are awfully good."

Luckily, the young business man treated this rather odd behaviour as a joke and replied: "What an enormous pile of food! I really don't know what to choose. I suggest you go back to your desert island, or wherever you came from, and bring me a bunch of bananas or some bread fruit."

Paul was mortified when he realised the tray was empty and, hardly noticing that the young man was laughing, cried, "Oh gosh! I am sorry," and retreated once more to the hatch, where he was told by the cook that his face was dirty. By seven o'clock he was feeling very downcast; he wished that he had not come in fancy dress; he wished that he could make conversation like Lucien; he wished that he could go home. Then, as all the guests seemed to be gaily eating, drinking and talking, and in the hope of forgetting his dissatisfaction, he started to compose a poem about the people in the room. He was searching his brain for a word to rhyme with *dowdy* and *rowdy*, when he heard a voice at his elbow, "Hallo, and what are you doing all alone, Mr. Pirate?" The owner of the voice was a middle-aged woman in tweeds and a dim felt hat, who looked as though she should not be at this party at all.

"I've been trying to be a waiter," said Paul.

"Oh really, how exciting. What a good idea to wear those lovely trousers and what *beautiful* shoes. Aren't you proud of the buckles?"

"They're not mine. My clothes are crumpled, so I borrowed these. I had to come in something."

"Of course you did," said the lady in tweeds soothingly. "Where do you come from?"

"About a mile away—no, a little bit more. We live in a white farm-house. Daddy says it's Georgian and Tibbles—she's our nurse—told Lucien that she shouldn't wonder if there was a ghost in it—not headless or clanking chains or anything, but just creeping around at night and slamming doors. Lottie—she's one of my sisters—is going to sit up when she's a little bit older and see if she can catch it."

"But how terribly thrilling for you. You must be a *very* brave boy. I should be simply terrified. What's your name?"

"Paul Edwin Trent Pennyfield."

"Goodness gracious, what a mouthful. Well, Paul, I want to ask you to do me a favour. Will you let me paint you in the costume you are wearing now?"

Paul hesitated. Was she joking? he wondered, but her expression was serious. She did not look or talk like an artist, in his opinion.

"Do you mean sit for you?" he asked in polite accents.

"Yes, that's it—sit for me. I live about a mile from here and I've got a lovely comfy studio."

"I'm not very good at sitting still."

"Of course not. It would not be right if a young and healthy boy like you didn't want to run around, would it? I shan't ask you to keep still for long. You look so picturesque in that lovely costume, I want to start on my picture this very moment."

"Do you paint with oil paint or water colours?"

"Oh, water colours. Do come—just to please me."

"All right," said Paul.

He told her his telephone number and she said she would ring him next morning and settle times and that she would be able to fetch him in her car, as she had quite a reasonable amount of petrol.

Chapter Twelve

THEY were walking home.

"But Paul, didn't you even mention payment?" asked Marie.

"I forgot all about money. I'm sorry; I was thinking that she didn't look like an artist, wearing that long heavy coat and skirt."

"Oh dear, I suppose she wants you to sit for nothing. I hate being mercenary, but it does seem awful when you think of all the digging and the window cleaning you could be doing during all the hours you're going to be in her studio. It isn't even as though she's a great painter," grumbled Marie. "We'll never be able to buy horses, canoes, or anything at this rate."

"Do stop fussing," said Lucien. "She'll probably give Paul a handsome present. Anyhow, I don't see why he shouldn't sit for her if he wants to. You really are becoming awfully mean—terrified that you might do something for nothing or waste time."

"It's all very well for you to talk, but it *is* disheartening when I try *so* hard to make money and nobody co-operates. It would have been so easy for Paul to say something about charges."

"There's time yet; he can mention it when she rings up. As for not co-operating, wasn't it I who arranged for us to stay to-night and wash up and make an extra five bob? Or am I mistaken?"

This remark was received in silence and the silence lasted until they reached their home and found Tibbles, waiting for them in the kitchen, with soup, and eggs, and bread and butter for supper.

No jobs were offered to them the next day, nor the day after, nor the day after that. Not even Paul's "lady in tweeds" rang up. And Lucien's pupil went away to stay with an aunt.

Lottie's temperature went down and she was able to get up for lunch on the day after the cocktail party; she spent the afternoon making a hoop for Cockade to jump through in the circus. Charles divided his time between reading, helping Tibbles and training Dandylion. Jennet gardened, wrote a one-act play for the variety show, wrote *The Story of Spookie* for the magazine and learned *The Charge of the Light Brigade*. Sheila answered another advertisement of bee-hives, read *Eric, or Little by Little*, and made a toy lamb. She was still in bed and unable to garden.

Paul exercised the tortoises, the ferrets and the mice, learned *The Ballad of East and West*, read *Treasure Island* and helped Tibbles. Marie wrote an article on *The Art of Driving Donkeys*, cleaned out the hen-house, shopped in Kingham and packed up some books she thought they might sell. Lucien started to make a theatre for Sheila's puppets, tried to teach Janet and Judas to come when they were called, mended the tailboard of Dandylion's cart and unpacked Marie's parcel of books, because he thought they should not be sold.

Then, three days after the cocktail party, new opportunities for making money arose. First, Miss Frankie White's novel—*In Search of Love*—which was written in the same handwriting as the letter, arrived. And, as though this was not enough to raise their hopes, when Lucien and Marie started to read it, the telephone bell rang and, within ten minutes, Jennet had fixed a job for the ferrets—they were to go ratting in the afternoon—and then the telephone rang again and this time it was the "lady in tweeds" asking if she could collect Paul for the first sitting at eleven o'clock. Paul forgot to mention the charges and said that would be fine.

This rapid business was followed by a good deal of discussion. Eventually it was arranged that Lucien, Marie, Jennet and Charles should go on the ratting expedition. Sheila did not want to accompany them, because she was squeamish and disliked bloodshed and disapproved of all blood sports. Anyway, Tibbles thought she ought to stay indoors and she wanted to type. Paul had accepted an invitation from the "lady in tweeds" for lunch and Lottie was forbidden to go by Tibbles, because she might get cold 'anging around.

Accordingly, at half-past one four Pennyfields, two ferrets and Cockade, whom Charles insisted on bringing, because long ago in her youth she had killed a rat, started on the two and a half mile walk to Babbington-under-Titwood. As they walked, they discussed Paul's birthday, which was in six days' time. Marie wanted to join up with Lucien and Sheila and give him *The Oxford Book of Victorian Verse*; but Lucien said Paul was not old enough to appreciate it and they should *all* combine and give him a duck and a drake. Jennet said, "Jolly good idea," and Marie wondered what the cost would be. Charles said Lottie and himself *had* decided ages ago to give Paul an exercise book and two pencils.

While they talked, the sun came out and shone golden on the wooded hills before them, on the dark and twisty road, on the spring hedgerows and the pale primroses in the cottage gardens. And Marie felt suddenly happy, so happy that she burst into song, which was an unusual occurrence; she sang "The Sweet Little Café" and "If You Would Only Come With Me" and "The Skye Boat Song" and "Keep Right On to the End of the Road." And then they reached the top of the hill and, with trees either side of them, looked down into the valley, where the little village of Babbington-under-Titwood sprawled in the sunlight.

"Oh, isn't it lovely," cried Marie. "Don't the cottages look sweet, like toy ones? And isn't the sky wonderful, so blue? I wish it was spring for ever and ever."

As the Pennyfields descended, they spotted their port of call—Lower Titwood Farm. There was no mistaking it because there were no other farms in the village—not that *it* was really more than a small-holding, having only a barn, a tumbledown cow byre and a few acres of wet, inadequately fenced land.

"Just the place to harbour rats," remarked Marie.

"I shouldn't wonder if there were some in the house as

91

well as the barn," said Lucien, knocking at the back door.

A dishevelled, stuttering woman, wearing a greasy over-all, answered their knock and presently, they understood all her explanations and directions and were able to fetch the barn key and start work.

The barn was large and airy. Inside were a few bales of damp straw, two trusses of musty hay and about a score of sacks, some filled with corn and others with old potatoes. As the children entered, they saw a rat scuttle away into the darkness of a corner. On looking, they found several holes in the back of the barn and Marie thought that some of them might be passages leading to the pit behind.

"Let's block them up or stand by them and then let Janet and Judas loose," she whispered.

"I'll hold Cockade by one," said Charles, "then she can kill the rat as it tries to run in."

'Right-o. Have you all got your sticks? Don't hit a ferret by mistake," said Lucien. "Shut the door, please, Jennet."

The children placed themselves carefully and Marie and Lucien took Janet and Judas from their pockets and dropped them gently on the floor, close to a bale of straw. Cockade let forth an excited yap and Judas sat down and started to scratch. Janet crawled behind the straw. The next moment a rat appeared and dashed in Marie's direction. Jennet gave a view-holloa and left the hole, which she was guarding, to hit at him with a stick. Cockade escaped from Charles and bounding forward received Jennet's hit, but ran on without faltering.

Lucien yelled, "Careful," and Marie kept her heel in her hole and struck out with her stick. The rat turned, Cockade pounced, and it was all over. A second later the terrier was shaking the rat vigorously in the proper and approved manner.

"Hurray, three shillings," said Marie.

"Oh, clever, *clever* Cockade," cried Jennet.

"I think she's the cleverest animal we've got," said Charles.

"It's a good thing you brought her," remarked Lucien, persuading Cockade to drop the rat.

"For goodness' sake, stick to your hole and don't hit her again, Jennet," said Marie.

After they had moved the bales and persuaded Janet to look in every corner, they decided to inspect the walls. They found that, like their granary at home, the barn was lined with wood to a height of about six feet and that the holes were entrances to the space between the lining and the wall.

"A paradise for rats," said Marie. "I should think there are hundreds and I don't see how they can escape. Wouldn't it be marvellous if we killed a hundred?"

"We must be careful and methodical," said Lucien.

"Let's have a walk round and see if there are any holes in the outside walls. We don't want the rats to dash out and disappear in the pit."

Lucien's forethought was well rewarded; they found three large holes and blocked them with some old pieces of tin and flints. Then, very excited, they returned to the barn and while the other children took their places once more and waited with raised sticks, Lucien carefully dropped Janet and Judas behind the wooden lining.

For a few moments nothing exciting happened. They could hear the ferrets running along and Cockade whined. Presently, looking very sweet, Janet peeped out of a hole and was nearly hit on the head by Marie. Then she continued on her way and soon the children heard a thump, thump, thumping noise ahead of her, which, according to Marie, could only be a rat.

"Gosh, it's running fast," yelled Charles.

"They're coming towards *me*," shouted Jennet, kneeling down and putting her eye to the hole.

"Don't do that, you idiot. We want the rat to come out there, so that you can hit it on the head," called Lucien.

Hardly were the words out of his mouth before they heard the sounds of a scuffle.

"She's killing it," shrieked Charles.

"Sssh! you'll upset Janet if you make such a row," warned Lucien.

"Where's that lazy old Judas, I should like to know? He's not half so clever as Cockade," said Charles.

"Here it comes, here it comes, it's nearly at me,"

shrieked Jennet. "Oh, now it's past. Look out, Charles, it's going towards you. Be ready. Quick, Charles. I'm sure you're not attending."

"Shut up, I am," said Charles, looking very serious and very anxious, and then he added: "Anyway, it's gone past now, just that moment. Look out, Marie!"

But the rat went past Marie and round all the holes again and then suddenly ran out of a hole by Lucien's feet, which nobody had seen. Lucien sprang forward and hit it on the head. Charles released Cockade, who dashed across the barn yapping loudly and was seized by the throat by an excited Janet. The moments that followed were terrible. Lucien and Marie pulled and tugged at the ferret without success. Jennet shrieked hopeless suggestions and Charles began to cry.

"She'll be dead soon; it's her jugular vein. She'll bleed to death," he moaned.

Cockade seemed powerless and merely tried to dash round and round the barn yelping. Soon a thin trickle of blood ran down her white coat.

"She's dying," shouted Charles.

"Hit Janet, hit her really hard. I will if you won't," cried Jennet.

"Oh, you are feeble. What will poor Lottie say?" said Charles.

Marie held Cockade and Lucien tried to pull Janet's jaw's apart, but he tried in vain. The little ferret clung on to the terrier's pink skin as though she would rather die than release her terrible grip.

Suddenly Jennet remembered the sentence she had read in the appendix of a book on dogs. It had been stored away in her memory and forgotten; now it came back to her. . . . *To make a ferret release his grip, tickle the toes and stomach with a stick.* A *stick*! She had one in her hand, but it was too big.

She ran into the field and saw, to her relief, a fallen tree at the far end. Reaching it, she broke two twigs from its dying branches and ran back to the barn. The door was shut; she pulled with all her strength; it came open suddenly and she nearly fell backwards. She grabbed a loose board in the adjoining wall to save herself; it came away

94

Lucien sprang forward and hit it on the head.

with her hand; she dashed into the barn. Lucien and Marie were still struggling. "Quick!" she shouted. "Out of the way, please."

"What is it—another mad idea?" asked Marie wearily.

"*Please*, Lucien, move," said Jennet, and the urgency in her voice made her brother leave go of Janet and step to one side. Jennet threw herself on the ground and with the shortest of her twigs started to tickle the ferret's toes.

"What *are* you doing?" asked Marie, still holding Cockade firmly by the collar.

The ferret began to squirm and Jennet seized and held her still with one hand, while she continued to tickle her toes and pinky stomach with the other.

"She's loosening her grip," said Lucien.

"Hurray," cried Charles.

"Let go, you little wretch," ordered Jennet.

The ferret squirmed and then, as Cockade flung up her head, swung, hanging on with her teeth. Jennet ran the twig along her stomach again and then, a second later, the ferret dropped to the ground and was grabbed by Lucien. Marie picked up Cockade. "Oh, that was terrible," she said.

"Is she all right?" asked Charles anxiously, peering at the terrier's neck.

"I'm just looking. She's not bleeding to death anyway," answered Marie.

"That was very clever of you, Jennet. Where did you get the idea?" asked Lucien.

"Read it—quite a long time ago."

"You deserve a medal," Marie told her. "Cockade's all right. It's only a nasty little wound."

"Let me have her. Poor, poor little dog. I hate Janet, *hate* her now. I shall never take her for another walk—beastly ferret," said Charles.

"Don't be silly. It's only Nature," said Marie.

"We must buck up and get on with this ratting. Who'll take Cockade into the house and bathe her neck?" asked Lucien.

"Jennet?" suggested Marie.

"Need *I* miss all the excitement?" asked Jennet.

"I'll come with you if you like," said Charles.

"Oh, all right, thank you," said Jennet.

"Don't be long, because we need you to stand at the holes," said Lucien.

"Don't chase out all the rats before we get back, please," said Jennet.

The two youngest of the ratters disappeared with Cockade, and Lucien put the two ferrets behind the wooden lining of the barn again. A rat dashed out of a hole almost immediately and Marie missed him with her stick. Janet was slow in pursuit and, by the time she had appeared, the rat had gone through the hole which Charles had been guarding earlier, and was behind the lining again. The next time it was Judas who brought him out into the open and Lucien who killed him.

"Six bob," said Marie.

"You are horribly bloodthirsty—— Sssh, Janet's after something," whispered Lucien.

He proved to be the last rat of the day and Janet killed him as he tried to run out through Marie's hole. Lucien put the three dead rats into an old tin bucket. Jennet, Lottie and Charles suddenly became squeamish and turned their backs and refused to come near the corpses.

After allowing the ferrets to explore the pit for a while, Lucien and Marie took the bucket to the house and showed it to the woman in greasy overalls. She gave a scream of horror and then, controlling her feelings, stammered congratulations. She was very tactless and did not mention paying the children, but stuttered, "Well, th-th-thank y-you very much. G-g-good-bye."

But Marie stood her ground and at the third good-bye said, "The charge will be nine shillings—three shillings per rat, as advertised, please."

Then the woman stammered that she had no change, but they could have her ten-shilling note and keep the extra. Lucien, however, produced two sixpences.

Chapter Thirteen

ON their way back to Scholar Farm they met one of Lucien's ex-friends—a boy of fourteen named Raymond George. He lived two miles from the Pennyfields in Upper Titwood House, which was large, sumptuous and Georgian, with a miniature park, excellent stabling and a walled garden. Jennet had never quite forgiven Lucien for ending the friendship, partly because Raymond owned two brown hunters; partly because he kept a canoe and partly because there were peaches and strawberries in the walled garden.

Now, when she saw Raymond coming towards them, broad, fair and self-assured, she felt her hopes rise. Perhaps he would invite the whole family to a party. Jennet loved parties.

"Raymond," she hissed.

"All right," her brother replied, "I'm not blind." He was feeling untidy and dirty, not in the right mood to meet this prosperous and affected friend of the past, who walked up the hill with a hint of a swagger and wore grey flannels and a tailor-made Harris tweed riding coat. He looked at his three companions and noticed that Jennet had scratched her face, that Charles's complexion was temporarily disfigured by a smear of mud, which appeared at first glance to be exactly like a little moustache, that Marie's dark hair was covered in hayseeds; and, at the sight of them, felt even more demoralised.

"Raymond's waving," said Jennet.

"Lucky you," said Marie.

"He's got awfully fat," remarked Charles.

Raymond said, "Good evening, Mr. Pennyfield, and what are you doing with all your little brothers and sisters, may I ask?"

"Killing rats. I haven't seen you for ages," replied Lucien.

"What a terrible occupation. I'm very well, thank you. Did you get any shooting last year? We went to a pukka place in Perthshire—fourteen guineas a week—wizard bar, dancing and everything."

98

"I haven't got a gun unfortunately, and, at the moment, we can't afford to take holidays," said Lucien.

"How are your horses?" asked Jennet.

"Oh, I don't know; I've hardly looked at them lately—out at grass, I expect—now the hunting season's over. We had one or two fine runs in December, but, of course, our pack's not up to much—a bit slow for my liking," answered Raymond, thrusting his hands into his pockets.

"You never met our ferrets, did you? May I introduce you to—Janet—Judas?" As he spoke, Lucien pulled a ferret out of each pocket.

Raymond stepped backwards. "Gracious, what hideous objects. How can you carry them about with you, Pennyfield? They must stink to high heaven. By the way, it's *not* you or your family, is it, who have put all those comic postcards in the post office?"

"Yes, it most certainly is," said Lucien firmly.

"Oh *no*, the whole village has been laughing over them—The Scholar Farm Wish Wash Service, The Scholar Farm Fetch and Carry Service—It *can't* be you, Pennyfield." Raymond's voice had become faintly mocking.

Marie laughed. "That's us," she said. "Do you want to give us a job?"

Silently, Lucien praised her self-possession. For a fleeting second Raymond looked a little embarrassed; then, recovering his self-assurance, he said with a casual air, "If one of your little brothers or sisters likes to clean my bicycle up, I would give them a sixpence or two. I'm going to sell it."

"No, thanks, we don't care for bicycles," said Charles.

"Not quite in our line," said Lucien; "thank you."

"But you are not really going round cleaning windows, are you, Pennyfield?" asked Raymond incredulously.

"Yes, and up to date, we've earned between four and five pounds. It's rather funny the jobs we get. The other day we acted as waiters at a cocktail party which was tremendous fun," said Lucien, throwing Janet into the air and catching her.

"But don't you feel you're letting your father down?" asked Raymond."

"Of course not. He's not like yours, with just one child

99

to bring up, and when a man's got seven, he hasn't time to be stuck up and superior. Daddy approves of children being enterprising anyway," Marie said sharply.

"Being enterprising is one thing and sticking mad postcards up in the post office and going round washing windows another," said Raymond, clicking his lead on to the smart collar of his pedigree cocker spaniel.

"You sound like a school marm," said Charles.

"My dear little boy, why don't you ask your nanny to teach you some manners and keep your face clean?"

"It's better to have a dirty face than swank like you," shouted Jennet.

"You're not worth arguing with. Good-bye, Lucien. Don't break your neck trying to be enterprising. I'm sorry for you living with so many brats. I mustn't be late back —going to see a show in London to-night."

With a smile Raymond left them and started to climb the hill which the Pennyfields had just descended.

"Beast! " said Charles.

"I hate him," cried Jennet. "And I don't believe he ever looks at those horses. He doesn't deserve to be so rich."

"Wasn't he horrible about hunting?" said Marie.

"He's not worth thinking about," said Lucien. "He's incredibly stupid, hardly managed to pass his common entrance and probably only swanks because he is suffering from an acute inferiority complex."

Lucien wondered whether the whole village was *really* laughing over the carefully worded Scholar Farm postcards and whether he and his brothers and sisters would ever manage to earn enough money to buy and keep a pony. Jennet wondered whether rats went to heaven.

They reached home in silence and found Sheila nearly in tears seated at their father's typewriter.

"It's all going wrong and I've worn a hole, with rubbing, through two pages and now the ribbon won't work," she said.

"Oh, cheer up. I'll have a try after tea. Where's Paul?" asked Lucien with false gaiety.

"Oh dear, I don't know; he came in and went out again. I think he's in the orchard. Lottie's helping Tibbles. Do you think I've broken the typewriter?"

"I'll see after tea. Didn't Paul say anything about the lady in tweeds?"

"No, I didn't ask him. I was too busy."

"I'm going to find Lottie," said Charles, "and tell her about Cockade." He ran down to the kitchen.

Filled with curiosity, Lucien and Marie hurried out to the orchard, where they found Paul lying beneath an apple tree, gazing at the sky.

"Hallo," he said. "Did you kill any rats?"

"Three. But what about you? Was it awfully funny?" asked Lucien.

"No, not frightfully. The picture's going to be awful— very wish-washy and ladylike. I had a jolly good lunch, though—chicken and brussels sprouts and rhubarb tart and cream. And then she insisted on buying me an ice-cream on the way back."

"Did she pay you?" asked Marie.

"Pay me? No."

"Didn't you mention charges?"

"Of course not. I can't go round asking everybody for money," answered Paul, rising to his feet and stretching.

"It's usual to pay people if you ask them to sit for you," said Marie.

"Nonsense, lots of people pay to *have* their portraits painted. I've been writing a poem. Could you possibly read it and see if it's suitable for the magazine? But let me get right away first; I'll go and help with tea," said Paul, and he ran out of the orchard.

"It is unfair," said Marie. "I don't see why I should always have to ask for the money. Paul's as bad as Raymond—going around being proud and pretending he doesn't need it. It's just silly to waste hours sitting for that woman; if the picture was going to be a great work of art, it would be an entirely different thing. I don't want to be mercenary, but if we all behave like Paul, none of us will have ponies or guns or anything."

"Look, let's forget money for a few hours. It's a wonderful evening. I could sit here and gaze at that cherry blossom with the blue sky behind it for an age, for countless ages. We are lucky that we have not been born in slums and that we have not lost our legs in an air raid. We are lucky to have this orchard and Dandylion and the dogs. We are lucky that we do not talk and look like Raymond. What's Paul's poem? Is it any good?"

"Much better than usual, I think. Wait a minute, though; I haven't finished reading it."

Lucien plucked a blade of grass and chewed it and then Marie said, "I wish I could write poetry. Do you think Paul would mind if you read this?"

"Well," answered Lucien, "if it's going in the magazine, every one will see it in the end."

"I don't think he would mind. Here." Marie handed him the sheet of typing paper on which Paul had scribbled his poem. Lucien read:

"Long, long I linger, here beneath the trees;
The dew-wet grass is damp against my cheek,
But what can it mean to me, this or these
Loveliest signs of spring, that rapturous speak,
With all the beauty of a lovely land?
Sunshine and the gentle swaying of the boughs,
And the young grasses, that like a hand
Touch my face, and the lowing of the cows,
Who have lost their calfs, sad as I,
Who have lost my friends, the yellow beaked,
Who oft here in the shade would lie
Quiet for a moment, content unseeked
By misfortune or despair; cheery-hearted,
Happy people with flat webbed feet,
Who now, by night mysterious, have departed;
Left their yellow house, their grassy beat
And faded into nothingness and are no more,
No more! The very sound calls forth a cry.
To action! Lie not beneath the sad wet trees.
It is not right that these two ducks should die,
Struck down and taken silently, to please
Some cruel being greedy for his meat.
Search, search the land and track the thief,
The murderer, the butcher of webbed feet.
This is no time to pause and bend to grief.

Chapter Fourteen

THE next day many exciting things happened. Firstly, Tibbles received a telegram to say that Mr. Pennyfield would be home in three days. Secondly, Lucien and Marie decided to collect the tools which the twins had left behind on their weeding expedition. Thirdly, a farmer rang up and asked whether *The Scholar Farm Useful Service* could take a pig to market on the day after next. But several depressing things happened too. Lottie spilled ink over the typing Sheila and Lucien had done the night before. Tibbles told the children that they must help more with the housework. Charles dropped a tray and broke three glasses and Spookie stole the meat that was meant for lunch.

The children were very excited over the telegram, but Tibbles was very severe. She warned them again and again that when their father came home they must "mind their p's and q's." She ran up and down and round and round, polishing furniture, dusting, sweeping and bustling everybody. It was not until the afternoon that the children eventually managed to escape from housework. Then Sheila sat in the sun and tried to type, Jennet, Lottie and Charles held a jumping competition on the lawn and Paul weeded the drive. Lucien and Marie collected the dogs and set out in the direction of Scholar's Water.

It was a damp day and cold for the time of year. There was a faint drizzle and the children kept their hands in their pockets. Brockie and Cockade were on leads, but Soloman, who was a well-mannered dog, walked at heel without a lead. The circular drive described by the twins was unmistakable and there were patches of gravel where the weeds had been pulled up. "What a beastly place!" said Lucien, knocking at the front door which the little dark man with the big beak-like nose opened.

"Good afternoon," said Lucien. "You may remember two children, who weeded some of your drive and lost a mouse here about ten days ago. Well, they left behind a small trowel and fork, and I wondered whether we could collect them now. I'm the children's brother, you see."

The man gave a cackle, which was so like Charles's imitation of it, that Marie wanted to laugh.

"Oh, you are, are you, young man? Very like the boy, too. I remember they lost a mouse in my shed. I don't know where the tools would be. I haven't seen them. Are you sure they weren't taken home?"

For a moment neither Lucien or Marie could answer, because Charles's mimicry of nine days ago had been so clever that they could barely suppress their giggles. After a short silence Lucien made a choking noise, recovered his self-control, and said: "No, we are certain that they are here, absolutely certain."

"I'm so sorry we are bothering you," added Marie.

"Shall we have a look round the garden? Perhaps they've got left in a border or something." Her voice trailed off as she caught Lucien's eye and started to giggle again.

"Yes, perhaps that would be best; meanwhile I'll look in the shed."

None of the garden seemed cultivated, so the children unleashed the dogs to run at will, and then wandered down the overgrown paths and poked the nettles with sticks.

Suddenly their attention was attracted by Cockade, who dashed past them with a secretive expression on her face, the sort of expression she always wore when she had found a bone or a ball.

"What's she got?" wondered Marie.

"Better have a look," said Lucien, "in case it's something splintery or poisonous."

They shouted and whistled until Cockade returned to them, crawling on her stomach in the most ridiculous manner. Lucien opened her mouth and removed the yellow foot of a duck.

"Gosh!" exclaimed Marie. Normally such an incident would mean nothing to them, but because of Flippy and Flappy's mysterious disappearance it seemed very important. The next moment Brockie appeared from the back of the house simply smothered in white feathers.

"He doesn't seem to keep hens or ducks himself," said Lucien, unknowingly voicing Marie's thoughts. "Quick, let's look further," he added, after a pause of a few seconds.

Possessed by a mingled feeling of curiosity and excitement, they ran round to the back of the house. By the shed they saw the man with the large nose setting fire to a pile of feathers, a pile which could not be seen from the road or drive.

"He's busy. Let's slip down to the shed," whispered Lucien. They were wearing gym shoes, but the man heard them as they reached the door.

"Well, have you found the tools?" he asked.

"No, I can't think *where* they can be," replied Lucien, peering into the shed.

The man looked at him sharply. "Well, they are not in there, young man. I've searched."

"Oh dear. Daddy will be so cross when he hears they are lost," said Marie, with an admirable attempt to appear sorrowful.

The man suddenly burst into a fit of cackling which made the children jump. "By Jove!" he cried. "Bless me if I didn't forget to give your little brother and sister their bit of brass after all. How much was it they wanted? Half a crown, I believe. Well, here's a pound, that will cover their labour and the loss of the tools. Now, hurry up and go home before your mother starts worrying. I know how these poor mothers suffer from their youngsters' pranks."

He handed Lucien a note and added, with another cackle, "You must be treasurer." The two children thanked him politely and asked him if he was sure that it wasn't too much, then called their dogs and left.

When they were out of earshot of the house, Lucien said, "Marie, that shed had a mass of packing cases in it and there was a large needle on the floor for trussing up chicken. Do you suppose those cases were filled with stolen fowl?"

"Who can say?" answered his sister. "If they are, that man has got to get rid of them. We must keep a watch on the house, I suppose, if we want to be clever."

"He looks cunning and dishonest in a way," mused Lucien.

"He wanted to get rid of us pretty quick. I should think those packing cases would travel by night. We had better not mention our suspicions to the twins and Jennet or we'll have them dashing off in strange cars again."

"It's a pity, when one remembers that the twins were the first people to make his acquaintance," said Lucien.

"Wouldn't it be wonderful if we caught the thieves red-handed?"

"Butt was saying that twenty January hatched pullets were pinched eight miles from here a week ago," said Lucien.

When they arrived home they found Tibbles trying to type *In Search of Love*, Sheila laying tea and Jennet and the twins helping Paul with the drive, which they hoped to have weedless by the time their father returned. Every one seemed very gay; the gramophone was in the front porch and, now and then, Jennet broke off to put on a record to cheer her companions at work. Lucien and Marie appeared on the scene to the strains of "The Road to the Isles." Sheila, seeing them from the lawn, shouted, "Did you find my fork?"

Marie said, "No, unfortunately not." And then Lottie and Charles stopped weeding to insult the man with the large nose. When they had exhausted their small vocabulary of adjectives, Lucien told them about the pound. And Marie told the twins that they shouldn't jump to conclusions.

Presently all the children went in to tea and, at tea, Tibbles said something which made Lucien and Marie sit up very straight and catch each other's eyes. She said, "Fancy, Mr. Bennet lost some of his chickens last night. Six ten-week-old pedigree pullets, four of last year's cockerels and a few laying fowl. It's getting terrible. You take care to shut everything up properly to-night. They say Constable Watkins and another policeman—one of the 'ead ones, I should think—have been looking for car tracks down our lane. It's about time they caught them, too. Really, I don't know what England's coming to now-adays, that I don't—what with all these murders, train accidents and fires. It's not safe to do anything, that it isn't."

After tea had been washed up, Lucien and Marie called Sheila and Paul into consultation and told them about the duck's foot and the bonfire of feathers. Paul wanted to watch the house of the man with the large nose all night. He wanted to take a camera and to take photographs of every one who visited the house. He said there would be a fine moon.

Sheila wanted them to start watching early in the evening, so that they should see the man with the large nose set out on his evil errand, and shadow him. At the same time, she was not sure whether it would not be better to put the whole affair in the hands of the police. Lucien and Marie said that if the police were any use at all they would have caught the thieves before now. Eventually a plan was made that two of the children should watch the house and that two should stand at the end of the lane which led to it where it met the road. The two by the house would see the man with the large nose if he left and the two at the end of the lane would, they hoped, see anything the others failed to see or any lorry dumping its stolen goods in the hedge. It was arranged that Marie and Paul should be by the road and Lucien and Sheila by the house.

That evening at ten o'clock, as they took up their vigil, they felt tense and excited; but this feeling did not last. Sitting behind a hedge the other side of the lane to the house, Lucien and Sheila soon became bored; and, within an hour, Marie and Paul were playing the unwinding game in an attempt to make the time pass quickly. Although there was no moon, it was a pleasant night with a light south-westerly wind and just the hint of rain in the air.

"At least, we shouldn't get chills," Sheila whispered to Lucien. It was then a quarter to eleven and a moment later they saw a lorry coming towards them up the lane. They crouched down as the headlights shone in their faces.

"It'll go past the others at the top," whispered Lucien, and the lorry changed gear and grunted by the gate and the hedge, which hid the children, and on up the stony hill to the main road at the top.

"It was a removal van," said Lucien, rising to his feet; "Picketts and Co., or something like that."

"I saw a table in the back," said Sheila, "wonder what they are doing, moving furniture at this time of night. It can't be anything to do with the twins' friend, because it never even slowed up as it went past his house."

While Sheila talked, the two Pennyfields at the top of the lane were very excited; they could see the headlights of the removal van and, as the lane was rarely used and only led eventually to one old farm-house and a few labourers' cottages, they felt certain that the van must have dropped some goods or collected some goods from the man with the large nose.

Marie held her torch in her hand; she meant to take the number of the van; she had brought a pencil and note-book.

Paul thought of Flippy and Flappy, and he remembered: *Search, search the land and track the thief, the murderer, the butcher of webbed feet.* Suddenly, he hated the lorry driver. He forgot the advice of his brothers and sisters, forgot that they had decided that it was silly to get into strange vehicles, like Jennet. He only knew that he wanted to catch the man who had killed his ducks. And he still felt the same when the headlights came nearer and he saw that it was not an ordinary lorry but a removal van that was approaching him. And so, when it stopped before entering the main road, he sprang to his feet, grabbed the tailboard, and, as Marie cried his name, pulled himself on to his tummy; then, pressing down on his elbows and kicking his legs, he scrambled into the van and lay panting by the table. Marie, meanwhile, had failed to take the number, owing to her brother's rash and sudden act, and stood rooted to the spot. Presently, however, she collected her wits and decided to run down the lane and tell Lucien and Sheila of the calamity. Three brains are better than one, she thought, breaking into an easy jog trot. She found her brother and sister still hiding behind the hedge.

They were horrified to hear of Paul's act and inclined to blame her for neither stopping him nor taking the number of the lorry, but they could not think what to do about it.

"Oh dear, oh dear," said Sheila. "I do hope he doesn't get murdered or anything. Such a lot of dreadful things are happening nowadays. We can't go home without him. Tibbles will be furious and worried to death. Oh dear, why *must* he be so tiresome?"

"It's so silly when it was only a removal van. Still, I

suppose in a way it would be worse if it was the thieves' lorry. I mean your fears, Sheila, would be more justified —he might be murdered, as you suggest. As it is, I think he's pretty safe really, although I wish he had a bit of money on him," said Lucien.

"Let's go up to the top of the road," said Marie. "This place is getting on my nerves."

"Not like you to have nerves," remarked Lucien.

The three children walked up the lane, deep in thought. Sheila remembered how deceitful they had been, how cunningly Lucien had hurried the unsuspecting Tibbles to bed and felt ashamed. Lucien purposely refrained from letting his mind dwell on Paul and wondered whether he would get in the Foreign Office and whether his father had had a rotten time in Russia, for he guessed that his father had been behind the iron curtain. At the cross roads they stopped and took refuge behind a hedge. This is a pretty aimless, hopeless affair, thought Lucien. We ought to have collected more evidence before we came trapesing out in the middle of the night. But the next moment he changed his mind, for they saw the headlights of a powerful vehicle coming down the main road; at least they thought it was a powerful vehicle, but when it came nearer they saw that it was in reality a car with powerful headlights. It was coming very slowly; when it reached the end of the lane it stopped and a man in a dark blue coat stepped out.

"Well," he said, "I think that's all for the night. You should get to the Rose and Crown without any difficulty. If, of course, anything does arise, you'll have to dump them at my house again; but I would rather you didn't do that; it's too tiresome getting rid of the traces. And remember, if you get that job done to-morrow night there's a pretty bit of brass waiting for you; but whether Tom's ill or not, you've got to work on your own." Lucien and Marie recognised this voice—it belonged to the man with the large nose.

The driver of the car said, "Yes, sir, and after that I'm going straight. I'm going to chuck this job," and started the engine.

Marie and Lucien pushed their heads a little way through the hedge and, as the car drove away, switched on their torches and took the number. Sheila watched the man with the large nose start down the lane without turning his back. When he was out of earshot, Marie said, "Gosh!"

"The first job is to ring up the police, I should think," said Lucien.

"I quite agree," said Sheila.

"It'll take us at least a quarter of an hour to run home," suggested Marie.

"Do we know any one on our way who would let us use their telephone?" asked Lucien.

"Can't think of a soul," answered Marie.

"All right; let's knock up a stranger. We mustn't waste time," said Lucien, turning and walking in the direction of Scholar Farm. For about fifty yards there were only fields on either side of the road, then they came to a little red brick house. As they went through its brown gate the moon appeared and her light relieved Sheila, who was inclined to feel afraid of the dark, and disconcerted Marie, who thought of the blackness of the night as a friendly protector.

Their loud bangs on the door seemed to resound right through the house; it was eerie, it was horrible. Sheila looked behind her—just in case the man with the large nose was following with a revolver in his hand. After the banging there was silence and then suddenly a shrill voice rang out. "Who's there? what do you want?" it asked in frightened, unsteady tones.

"Sounds like an old lady," muttered Lucien, before shouting: "Can you let us in, we want to telephone the police quickly, please. It's all right; we're not thieves or murderers; we are children catching a thief."

Now they heard the voice call: "Geoffrey, Geoffrey." And presently a window opened and a grey-headed man peered out, looking exactly as Marie had always imagined Uncle Ebenezer in *Kidnapped* looked.

"What do you want at this time of night?" he asked in a husky, old voice.

"We want to dial 999 now, sir, if possible. We are relying on you to lend us your telephone."

Geoffrey—as the children called him afterwards—

looked suspiciously at them for a moment or two, before making up his mind and saying: "All right, I'll come down, but I don't call *you* a child."

"No, perhaps not, sir, although I *am* still at school," replied Lucien politely.

The grey head disappeared abruptly; the window shut, and then the children heard the shrill voice ask a question and the sound of someone coming down the stairs.

"Oh dear," said Sheila, "how long it seems since we left the lane. I'm sure the police will never catch the thieves now."

"Pessimist!" cried Marie. "Of course they will. I do think this is fun. I wonder what happens when you've dialled 999. I wish Jennet was here. She would be imagining our photographs in the paper already."

"It's a pity she's not older," said Lucien. "You know, I'm sure we wouldn't have half so much fun if we weren't poor. Think, Cockade wouldn't have found the duck's foot or Brockie the feathers if the twins hadn't tried to earn some money."

"Here he comes—Uncle Ebenezer," whispered Marie.

"Oh no! Uncle Ebenezer wore a night cap," contradicted Lucien.

Presently they heard bolts being shot back and then, slowly, carefully, the door was opened a few inches.

"Ah, now then—let's see you." The owner of the house stood before them, wearing an old cloth dressing-gown over striped pyjamas. His hair was on end and his feet bare. He looked very sleepy indeed and as though he normally wore spectacles, Marie thought.

"Well," he continued, "we don't want you *all* dialling 999. You two girls had better wait here in the hall while your brother does the telephoning. Who is this thief?"

"Thank you, sir, thank you very much. I'm awfully sorry to get you out of bed at this time of night. It's a car load of stolen chickens. We must catch them—*pro bono publico*—they've done a lot of damage round these parts," Lucien told his host, leaving Marie and Sheila and following him into the dining-room.

The two girls heard Lucien say: "Hallo, I'm speaking from the Scholar's Water, Thrushfield, Kingham Road,"

111

and then Geoffrey returned and started to question them on their activities. He seemed very curious. Sheila thought, especially for an old man. He wanted to know where they lived and how many dogs they kept, and whether they, the children, felt the cold; and whether they employed any servants and the age of their father. He told them a few facts about himself, though: that he had lived all his life in these parts, that his wife was an invalid, that he used to breed dogs, that he had never left England and that his only son had died at the age of ten.

Sheila was attacked by a violent attack of giggles. Geoffrey asked whether she was laughing at his appearance and Marie had to invent a mass of excuses. Luckily, Lucien came into the hall before she had exhausted her imagination.

"Well, it seems there's nothing for us to do but go home now," he said. And then, turning to Geoffrey, "Thank you very much for lending us your telephone. I do hope we did not startle your wife with our loud bangs and raucous yells."

"Oh no, she doesn't mind. Are they going to catch the thief? What did they say?"

Geoffrey was so obviously bubbling over with curiosity and he asked the question in such an odd manner, that Sheila began to giggle again. Lucien gave her a withering glance and said: "I'm not quite sure. I think they will cop the car all right. I've given them the number." Then he held out his hand, saying, "Good-bye, sir, and thank you again very much."

Out in the road once more, Marie said: "It's all very fine to go running home, but what about Paul?"

"Oh dear, we *must* do something," added Sheila.

"As far as I know, he's beyond our help at the moment. He may be in Manchester or Plymouth by now, or, alternatively, he may have jumped off at the traffic lights in Kingham and be nearly home by now. How can we search for him, when we haven't the foggiest notion where the removal van was going? I almost mentioned him to the police and then I changed my mind. We don't want to make fools of ourselves again—after the Jennet episode. I honestly don't think we can do any good. We'll just have to go home to bed and hope for the best," said Lucien.

"Let's *will* him to return swiftly and safely," suggested Marie.

And so, as the three children walked back in the moonlight, they muttered, *"Paul come home now, Paul come home now,"* over and over again.

Chapter Fifteen

DON'T worry, my friend,
For this is the end.
   You're going where others have been,
With little webbed feet
And faces so sweet,
   In the clutches of men that are mean.

For the first few miles Paul invented poetry. He felt ecstatic. This surely was adventure at last. The sight of the table did not really disconcert him at first, because up in the front of the van there were some packing cases filled —he decided—with stolen goods, probably dead fowl. After all, he reasoned—after he had been lying on the floor for nearly an hour—no innocent, law-abiding lorry driver would be out at this time of night.

It was the sight of the army huts on the common that changed his mind. Although occupied, they looked strangely derelict and suddenly Paul remembered that several children had been found murdered in different parts of the country last week and, at the same moment, he began to feel stiff and cold. All his courage left him. Instead of treading the thrilling path of adventure, he was being driven to his doom.

He started to think of the comfortable and the good things at home. He wished that he was safely in bed in his primrose and green room, that he had never ventured out at all.

Then, to make matters worse, the land was plunged into darkness. He moved to the front of the van and sat on a packing case, because he was feeling sick and did not want

113

to look out any more. He tried to invent poetry, but in vain. Where was he going? What would the driver do when he found him spying? What sort of man was the driver? Were Lucien, Marie and Sheila sick with worry? What would Tibbles say? How was he going to get home?

Paul asked himself these questions over and over again, but could find no answer. And as the seconds turned into minutes and the minutes turned into half-hours and the half-hours into hours, he found it increasingly difficult to keep his mind off the most dismal and depressing subjects. At last he started to recite poetry: *Drake's Drum, The Lady of Shallot, The Stolen Child*. He nearly cried when he reached:

> "Away with us he's going,
>   The solemn-eyed—
> He'll hear no more the lowing
>   Of the calves on the warm hill-side."

To stop himself he recited as much as he could remember of *The Charge of the Light Brigade* and *Bonnie George Campbell*, and these gave him heart. Then he realised that the removal van was entering the suburbs of a town; there were street lamps and shops and dreary pavements. Again he wondered where he was going and how he would return home.

Presently the driver took a side turning and, creeping to the back of the van once more, Paul saw that they were travelling along a series of back streets. As a clock struck the quarter hour, the van turned into a yard and stopped. The driver jumped out; a door opened; a woman called *cooeee*.

Then the sound of Cockney voices came to Paul—the woman's and the driver's. The woman asked what the driver had been doing out so late and why he hadn't left the lorry at the yard. The driver said he had been right over the other side of Kingham, fetching some furniture from the farm-house, when the old bus broke down; he couldn't find a garage within five miles and it took him a couple of hours before he managed to put the old girl to rights. He had lost his bearing twice on the way to the

114

house and arrived an hour late anyway; by the time he had got the furniture loaded—and that took long enough, what with Jack being ill and no one to help him—the people at the nearby cottage had taken pity on him and suggested he might like a bite of something before he started for home; and, seeing that he was hungry, he had accepted their invitation and stayed eating and drinking for a bit.

It was close on eleven when he eventually left and, guessing that the yard would be shut up and knowing that the toffs what owned the furniture would be in bed, he decided to come home, have a quick nap and then pop round with the furniture as soon as it was light. The woman said he had better think of some better excuses for that Mr. Parker and the driver said he had no need to; it was about time *they* overhauled the lorries. Then the two of them went indoors and Paul was left alone in the tiny yard.

For several minutes he sat very still, gazing at the light that shone through the curtains of what appeared to be the kitchen, regretting that he was such a coward. If only he had had the courage to leap out of the van and explain all, he might now be sitting in that kitchen drinking hot tea, instead of mouldering alone in this horrible van. But it was not too late now, he told himself; he could still bang at the door and attract their attention to his plight.

He was trying to sum up enough courage for this action when the light went out and, except for the dim yellow blur from the street lamp, the yard was plunged in darkness. They've gone to bed now, he decided. You're too late, Paul, as usual.

A few minutes later he was out of the van and climbing the yard gate. Lucien had taught him several things about climbing and he had spent many hours at home in the apple and oak trees.

Soon he was walking down the grey and dirty street, feeling that he was not Paul any more, but some fantastic character in a book. Now that he was on the move, he felt braver again. Gosh! wouldn't the others be surprised when they heard what he had been doing? He imagined himself recounting his adventures to them and was wishing that he possessed Charles's power of mimicry, when he saw the head of a policeman coming round the corner.

He only saw the head because they were walking down streets that ran at right angles to each other and the fence at the corner was about five feet in height. All the Pennyfields possessed a natural fear of policemen, because all the Pennyfields were in the habit of trespassing, quite harmlessly, and had once been caught poaching. Now Paul looked to right and left and saw, to his intense relief, a gap in the split oak fence at his side. In a moment he was through the gap and lying flat on his tummy. And then he saw the policeman's light flashing up the street and heard his heavy tread as he went by. Paul thanked providence that he had been in time and, after waiting a little while, ventured out again. After that incident he walked for several hours without meeting a soul. It was eerie, but so long as he kept moving he did not feel frightened. He tried to keep his mind on other subjects; he thought chiefly of his birthday and his father's return.

Then at last he saw, over the roof tops, the chimney stacks, between church spires and the factory funnels, the first grey streaks of dawn. Never before had he been so pleased to see the dawn; and presently, as he stopped and gazed at the eastern sky, he heard a cock crow and then suddenly this dim and murky maze of back streets seemed to come to life. Lights were turned on; curtains drawn back; dogs turned out to wander in the street. Night workers came bicycling or walking home, unshaven, sleepy-eyed. A milk van passed Paul and a postman on his way to the office. A costermonger left his squalid dwelling with a hand barrow of vegetables and flowers. And now Paul was worried. He wished that he had given himself up to the policeman after all.

It would be quite exciting to see inside a prison, he thought; but when, a few minutes later, he nearly ran into a tall constable of agreeable appearance, he was again unable to sum up enough courage to explain his plight or ask advice. And now, with the morning, came thoughts of his family at home. How worried they would be! How hard for poor Marie to describe his foolish act! If only he had some money; if only he hadn't given his half-crown to that beggar. Paul felt in his pockets, turned them inside out and found that he had twopence halfpenny and his knife,

Lucien had taught him several things about climbing.

which had been given to him by an uncle and was, according to Tibbles, worth a lot of money. There was something reassuring about the feel of his knife; it gave him heart and then it gave him an idea. At least the knife and a shop gave him the idea. He had entered a busier street, and was relieved for no particular reason to see a string of buses, when he noticed the name above one of the shabbier shops: *T. Rubens, Pawnbroker, Ealing.* And suddenly he knew his line of action. "I'll pop my knife," he said. (It was a phrase he had read in a book.)

And he stopped and looked at the shutters in front of the window. Then he leaned against them with his hands in his pockets and gazed across the yard. Only one shop seemed open—a baker's—from which came the lovely smell of baking bread. Paul realised that he was very hungry; in fact now he felt quite weak.

Grasping his three coins, he hurried across the road and bought two penny rolls of bread. To his disappointment, they were stale—or anyway yesterday's baking. He went back to the pawnshop and taking up his previous place, tried again to invent poetry. Then he noticed a newsagent, who declared on a blackboard outside his shop that he sold papers of the day before for wrapping for a halfpenny. And, a few minutes later, Paul, penniless, dishevelled and disreputable, was reading yesterday's *Daily Mirror.*

He regretted his purchase directly, because on the very front page was a guesome account of the murder of a little boy of ten. Hurriedly Paul turned to the middle page, only to see the photograph of a girl who had been found strangled in a London air-raid shelter two days ago. Yet although the grisly stories, so full of ghastly detail, filled him with horror, they possessed also a strong fascination and he felt compelled to read them. By half-past eight, however, he was tired of the *Daily Mirror* and impatient for the pawnbroker's shop to open; he was beginning to worry again, too, wondering whether Scholar Farm was in a terrible uproar. He was haunted by remorse now and the more he thought of Lucien's and Marie's difficult situation, the more angry he felt with himself for being the cause of it.

118

At last he could bear it no longer and decided to knock up the pawnbroker. Taking his knife from his pocket he gave the door three sharp taps and then stood back and waited expectedly. He thought he heard some movement upstairs, but no one appeared and so he tapped again and called "Mr. Rubens" twice.

A woman, wearing curlers, shouted from the next door house that she doubted that he was up yet; but Paul was not to be disheartened; he felt that he could wait no longer; the thought of the anxiety of his family was torture; with desperation there came courage. He banged the door and called the pawnbroker's name yet louder than before. Passers-by looked at him oddly, but he did not care. He wanted to go home now, at once. And then suddenly the door opened softly, slowly, making him jump, and there stood the pawnbroker in bedroom slippers and his shirt sleeves. Paul was determined to get first word in.

"I say," he said, "I'm terribly sorry to bother you, but I want to pop something. I'm in a frightful fix, and I ought to be in Kingham, which is miles from here—in Loamshire—and I've got no money at all. How much will you give me for this knife? My name is Paul Pennyfield."

Mr. Rubens looked him up and down—looked at his jacket, patched with leather at the elbows, looked at his grey flannel shorts, looked at his dark tangled hair and his comparatively new sandals.

"Well, Mr. Paul Pennyfield, I think you had better come inside," he said, and his voice was smooth, oily.

Paul saw in his mind's eye the face of the murdered ten-year-old boy; but squaring his shoulders he said, "Yes, sir," and walked in without hesitation. A moment later he wondered whether he should have called this man *sir*. Mr. Rubens switched on the light and darted behind the counter.

"Now will you let me see this knife, please?" he said.

With a pang of regret Paul handed it over, saying, "Tibbles—she's our nurse—thinks it's worth quite a lot."

"May I ask how you managed to get here from Kingham?—it was Kingham, wasn't it?" said Mr. Rubens.

"I was trying to catch the thief who stole my ducks," answered Paul. "Actually I live at Scholar's Water, which is about five miles from Kingham. How much *do* you think it's worth? I've got no time to waste."

"Nor have I," replied Mr. Rubens sharply. "You had better tell me a bit more about yourself before we start discussing how much this knife is worth to me."

"I only want enough money to pay my fare home. I expect Daddy will come and collect it pretty soon. Ten shillings would do."

"Listen, Mr. Paul Pennyfield. For all I know you may have stolen this knife; for all I know you may have escaped from a remand home. I am not in the habit of dealing with children and, before I do anything to help you, I want to know the truth and nothing but the truth."

Paul hesitated for a moment and then he said, "I'm not in the habit of stealing and I don't know what a remand home is; but I *can* tell the truth. About six days ago my two ducks, Flippy and Flappy, disappeared. . . ."

He raced through the story, for the longing for home was almost unbearable and he felt that if he had to wait many more minutes for the money he would simply give way and sit on the floor and cry. When he reached the end Mr. Rubens said, "Thank you. Now can you give me your address and telephone?"

At last, at last, thought Paul, and gabbled the information.

"Now just sit down a moment, will you? I won't be long." With these words Mr. Rubens came from behind the counter, locked the shop door and then went back and through into the room behind, where he started to telephone.

Sitting alone in the shop, Paul felt that his doom was sealed. The door was locked. The window was shuttered. He could not reach the busy street. To-morrow his photograph would be in the *Daily Mirror*. He would never see his father again; he would miss his own birthday. It was the thought of his birthday that brought the tears to Paul's eyes. He had been looking forward to it for so long. He was trying to overcome this wave of self-pity when he heard Mr. Rubens say, "Yes, I'll see him on to the train. The station's only about a hundred yards from here." There followed the familiar *ting* as the receiver was put

120

down and then Mr. Rubens came into the shop again.

"Well, Paul," he said, "I've fixed everything with your nanny; you won't half get a scolding when you get back. What is it you call her—Tibbles? Well, she's going to meet you at the station—Kingham— and I'm going to see you on the train here. So think yourself lucky that you've stumbled on a man like Mr. Rubens. Here's your knife. You had better come through and have breakfast with my wife and I. We are eating something rather good this morning, but not quite what the government would approve of, so keep quiet about it."

Silent and surprised, Paul followed small, hook-nosed Mr. Rubens into the bright, newly decorated room behind. After the dustiness and darkness of the shop it seemed incredibly light and clean.

Chapter Sixteen

"THIS is ridiculous. Where *is* Paul?" asked Tibbles.

They were standing in the dining-room; breakfast was on the old black dresser.

"I am sorry, but we don't know," Lucien said vehemently. And Marie added, "He arranged to sit for the 'lady in tweeds' this morning, so I should think he might be back soon."

"I'm so hungry. Can't we start without him?" wailed Charles.

"It seems to me we can't do much else. It's a pity you sleep so heavy. Any other child would have heard him go," said Tibbles.

They all sat down and poured milk and sugar on to the porridge, which Tibbles considered more nourishing than any "new-fangled cereal." The three adventurers of the night before gave each other uneasy and significant glances. They had decided to avoid mentioning their escapade, and, so far, it had not been difficult to keep to this decision. It was perfectly true that they did not know Paul's whereabouts nor whether he had meant to rise early this morning. But now, as they ate their porridge, they began to realise that soon they would have to confess all. They remembered only too well the fuss that had accompanied the search for Jennet. The more they turned the proposition over in their minds, the more they disliked it.

They felt that everything connected with last night had fallen flat. Lucien had told the others that the police did not seem particularly interested, that they had taken down the number of the car and his name and address, but with a reluctant tone.

This waiting for news of Paul was worse for him than the other two children, because he had work to do. Timothy's Latin exercises were in the nursery, uncorrected. Within an hour he should be at Thrushfield Manor hearing the third declension.

Lottie would not stop talking about Paul, although Marie nudged her under the table three times; she made the most fatuous suggestions as to his whereabouts, said Lucien should ring up the police and then wondered aloud whether Paul could have been run over.

"It's so strange," she remarked. "I mean Paul isn't like Jennet. He doesn't go whizzing off in cars. He's much too cautious. Do you think he might have gone climbing trees and slipped and fallen and broken his neck?"

"Oh, do shut up," said Marie sharply. "Why are you always so pessimistic?"

"There's no need to be so jolly disagreeable. I think it's jolly worrying—losing your brother. A real catastrophe. If nobody else will ring up the police I will soon."

"Will you mind your own business, Lottie? If Paul has not returned by nine o'clock, we will start searching, but ring up or see the police and make a fool of myself again, I will *not* do! Charles, sit up and eat properly. What your poor father will say about your table manners when he gets back, I don't know, that I don't."

"Sorry, Tibbles," said Charles.

After that they were silent, until suddenly the telephone rang, making them all jump, although Lucien had been waiting, hoping for it.

"There! " exclaimed Tibbles.

"He's had an accident," said Lottie.

"Shall I answer?" asked Marie.

122

"Yes, hurry along, child."

"Oh God, make Paul all right. Don't let him be dead, don't let him be dead," prayed Sheila.

"If he's been killed, I shall commit suicide," said Charles solemnly.

"Don't be stupid," said Tibbles sharply.

"He's probably having breakfast with the 'lady in tweeds,' " Jennet suggested cheerfully.

"If *that's* all he's been doing, I shall give him a piece of my mind, that I shall—causing us all this anxiety," threatened Tibbles.

"He will have only been trying to earn money," said Lottie.

Suddenly Jennet started to giggle and then her toast went down the wrong way and she started to cough and Lottie patted her on the back and started to giggle too. The next moment Marie called, "Come quickly, please, Tibbles. It's from London. A man named Rubens has got Paul, and he wants to speak to you."

Jennet became subdued at once. There was something ominous about the call having come from London—or so it seemed to the younger children. Tibbles put her napkin on the table and left the room without a word.

"We must really try to buy Paul his birthday present to-day," said Lucien.

Then Charles surprised them all by saying, "Oh, he is lucky."

"Why?" asked Lucien.

"Seeing London. I've always wanted to go there, *always*."

"But how did he get there?" wondered Lottie.

"I'll tell you," said Lucien.

Marie returned and, when Lucien had finished his explanation, she said, "It's all right. Somebody's lending him some money. The van took him to Ealing. He's just about to have breakfast."

Then Tibbles came back, very flustered, and, after she had given them a long lecture on deceit and the dangers of children wandering about at night, Lucien had to explain all over again.

At the end the nurse said, "Well, I *never*. Of all the

123

naughty children, I think you're about the worst, that I do. First Jennet and now Paul. Lucien, you ought to be ashamed taking out your younger brothers and sisters at that time of night. But there! You gets it from your poor father, I suppose." And suddenly to their amazement Tibbles burst out laughing, sat in a chair and laughed till the tears were rolling down her cheeks. "Young demon," she kept saying, "Young demon—gadding about London at his age."

"Oh, he *is* lucky," said Charles.

"I'll take you up to London one day," Lucien said.

"Honestly? Is that a promise?"

"If you really want to go. You may be disappointed."

"Me too," yelled Lottie.

"I can't take all of you."

"I don't want to go, thank you. I hate beastly smelly towns," declared Jennet.

"You're jealous," said Lottie.

"I'm not."

The telephone bell rang again; this time Lucien answered it.

"I bet it's the 'lady in tweeds,' " said Jennet.

But she was wrong. Lucien came back smiling all over his face. "I don't know what to do. It's a reporter from the *Kingham Star*. He wants to see us about last night. I told him that there was no real story in it, that we had done nothing; but he insists on coming—says he will be here about twelve, and there's no need for me to be modest."

For a moment every one was silent. Then Sheila said, "Oh dear." And all the children started talking at once.

"What are you saying *oh dear* about?" asked Marie. "I think it's marvellous."

"Oh, you lucky, lucky people. You'll have your photographs in the paper and everything," cried Jennet, knocking her plate on the floor.

"Why didn't you tell us you were going out last night?" asked Lottie.

"I don't really feel a bit excited," said Marie.

"I wonder what Daddy will think," said Sheila.

"Oh, it's so exciting," cried Lottie, and she started to dance round the table.

"It seems awful in a way. I mean that we've made people be cast into prison. I don't mind about the man with the large nose—it's the driver of the car; he had quite a nice voice," said Sheila.

"Oh, don't be such a wet smack," cried Jennet. "Why are you so stuffy? Let's be gay. This is a time for celebration, not regrets."

"Gosh, look at the hour. I've got to go and teach Timothy. I shall have to correct those wretched exercises on the way," said Lucien.

"You won't be back for the reporter. You *must* be here when he comes," Marie told him quickly.

"Yes, I shall. It's only an hour lesson."

"My Gosh!" cried Lottie. "What a catastrophe—here's the 'lady in tweeds.'"

"Hide," said Charles.

"I'm going to go and tell her about *everything*. I think she'll be jolly interested," shrieked Jennet.

"I'm off. I'm late anyway," said Lucien, running from the room.

Then Tibbles broke her long silence. "What *will* your poor father say about all this? I don't know, that I don't. Yes, Jennet, you had better go and explain—it's only polite. Well, I suppose I had best put on my hat and coat and catch the bus to Kingham. Fancy you finding them thieves! I hope Lucien 'asn't gone and frightened off the reporter-man. Lottie, your face is filthy, *filthy*; run upstairs and wash it and don't kick out the stair rods. Well, I must be off to meet that tiresome boy. Now, *mind* and get yourselves clean and tidy—Charles, don't bite your nails; there'll be nothing left soon—before twelve. Marie, you take care that no one gets into mischief and, if I'm late, put some eggs into bake for lunch and make a nice barley pudding—there's a duck."

When they had found Tibbles a basket, welcomed Butt, and cleared away the breakfast things, Marie, Sheila and the twins went to join Jennet in the orchard, where, seated on the fallen apple tree, she was talking to the "lady in tweeds." As she walked across the sunlit garden and through the little white gate, Marie felt happy and if any one had asked her why, she would not have been able to answer. The feeling was caused by so many things—the spring air, the sunlight, blue skies and the birds' singing, the early cherry blossom, the happiness of Tibbles and Marie's brothers and sisters, the fact that her father was coming home and, perhaps more than she realised, the fact that she was young and strong with years and years of life before her.

"I think it's awfully exciting—a real reporter. I do hope Paul will get back in time to be included," Jennet was saying, bouncing up and down on the tree. Then she saw Marie and cried, "Oh, here's the sister you saw at the cocktail party. . . . Marie, can I introduce you to Mrs. Buckrum."

"How do you do?" said Marie, laughing and shaking hands. "I'm afraid Jennet's been swanking. I'm frightfully sorry about Paul, though. It's awful that you should use your valuable petrol on a fruitless journey. We should have let you know. These are some younger members of the family—Lottie, Charles. And, oh, here's Sheila."

"How do you do?" muttered the other children.

"I think you are all wonderful, *simply* wonderful. Your father *will* be proud of you when he gets back," said Mrs. Buckrum, causing every one but herself great embarrassment. Jennet was the first to recover.

"You wouldn't have thought us wonderful if you had seen me knock my plate on the floor at breakfast," she said.

"Would you like to see some of our animals? I mean if you've nothing to do this morning," suggested Lottie.

"I should love to."

"I'm going to play the gramophone. This is a time for celebration. We *must* be gay," said Jennet, leaping from the tree.

"Cockade's the best dog; she catches rats." Lottie started to tell Mrs. Buckrum about the animals.

"Well, if you're going to do the cooking, Marie, I shall get on with *In Search of Love*. Tibbles was most expert; she typed three pages in an hour yesterday," said Sheila.

"What's this? Do you clever children *type*, too?" asked Mrs. Buckrum.

"Sheila tries to," said Marie; this flattery was getting on

126

her nerves, she decided that Mrs. Buckrum was a hypo-
crite.

"I'm terribly slow. It takes me about half an hour to do
one page properly. The writing's awfully difficult to read,"
explained Sheila.

"It's a terribly funny book. Nobody really falls in love
with anybody. And they haven't got any animals at all,"
said Lottie.

"When it's finished we are going to be paid a lot of
money," added Charles.

"Are you really? Now that *is* enterprising," said Mrs.
Buckrum.

"Ah, here's Dandylion; she shakes hands awfully well.
Someone gave her to us two years ago. She's very intelligent, not obstinate like some donkeys, and goes in the
cart, but only Lucien and Marie can really manage her
properly," Lottie went on.

"I'll fetch Tick and Tock," said Charles. As he ran away
across the orchard he started to play his mouth organ.

"I do think we ought to be gay," said Jennet, hurrying
indoors to fetch the gramophone.

"What a *sweet* donkey," exclaimed Mrs. Buckrum.

Chapter Seventeen

AT first Jennet thought the interview with the *Kingham
Star* reporter disappointing. He arrived at two o'clock instead of twelve o'clock, wearing a brown suit, rather dingy
brown shoes, a homburg hat, and spectacles. He was
small, in appearance insignificant, and possessed an un-
pleasing voice. When he had asked the children their
names, ages and schools, he said, "Well, tell me all about
it. How did you know these people had stolen goods in
the car?"

Lucien told the story once more, keeping it as short as
possible and starting with the disappearance of Flippy and
Flappy. Jennet cut in occasionally when she thought he
was underrating his intelligence and embellished it.

Then the reporter told them that the car had been

stopped on the Oxford-London road at about midnight and that the two packing cases were not filled with chicken, but with a much more valuable cargo—silver and a locked box of jewellery stolen from Upper Titwood House. This news caused great excitement amongst the Pennyfields. The children became much more talkative and, before any one could stop her, Lottie had told the reporter about Paul's trip to Ealing and her own trip in Mr. Phillips' car. Paul felt self-conscious and went out into the garden, and then Charles told the reporter about Paul's birthday and their plan to buy him some ducks.

"Yes, and we were going to try to find some this afternoon, because you said you were coming at twelve, and now—thanks to your extreme lateness—we are in the soup," added Jennet.

"Oh, we are not; don't invent," said Sheila hastily.

"Believe me, it wasn't my fault I was late, but I think your ideas are whizz-o, and, if you will allow me, I can be of some use. I've got one more port of call and, as luck would have it, I pass a farm which is swarming with ducks. So I can take some of you there in the old bus."

"Oh, thank you," cried Jennet.

"Bags I go," cried Lottie.

"What shall we tell Paul?" wondered Sheila.

"Surely one of you young genii can spin a convincing yarn?" suggested the reporter.

"Yes, I've thought of something," said Sheila.

"Oh, pretty hot, bang on!" exclaimed the reporter. "Now, tell me—where's your Popa? What does he do?"

"He's been abroad, be home soon and Mummy's dead," said Lucien instantly.

"Oh, hard luck! Is he in the army then? Must get him in the story, you know."

"It's secret," said Lottie.

"Oh well, never mind. Who looks after you?"

"Tibbles—I'll fetch her," answered Jennet.

"Have you a photo of yourselves?" asked the reporter.

"I don't think so," said Lucien.

"Yes, we have," contradicted Sheila. "I'll get it."

Tibbles was very flustered and not at all communicative. She was furious with the reporter, because he asked

her her age and birthplace; but cheered up when he began
to question her on the children; in fact, much to Lucien
and Marie's surprise, she actually began to swank about
them all.

"They're very good children really—get up to mischief
sometimes, but they wouldn't be healthy if they didn't.
And most of them are good at schoolwork. Lucien's got a
picture in his school exhibition and Marie won an essay
prize last term—ever such a nice book it was. She's good
at games too. Sheila got ever such a nice report and a
medal for good conduct and Lottie's clever at sums.
Charles won a reading prize two years ago—I taught him,
taught them all except Lucien. And Jennet—well, some
says Jennet's the brainiest of the lot, when she tries but
she doesn't try very often, talks too much. They all take
after their father. He's a clever man, very clever man."

Sheila interrupted at this moment, returning with a
photograph of all the children sitting on Mr. Bennet's wall.
As she showed it to the reporter, Jennet cried, "Oh no,
you can't give him that one. I look awful and I'm wearing
my spectacles."

And Charles said, "It's a beastly photograph. I look so
glum."

"And I've got a beastly smug smile," said Lottie.

"And Paul looks a prig," Jennet went on.

"Don't talk so silly, don't," said Tibbles sharply.

"I think it's very nice, don't you, Nanny?" said the
reporter, putting it in his pocket.

"Oh gosh! Here's the 'lady in tweeds' come for Paul.
Paul—Paul—Paul!" yelled Jennet.

"We had better go for those ducks, Mr. Reporter," said
Lottie.

"His birthday's in four days' time," added Charles.

"Well, I can't take more than six of you."

"Then, *six* of us would like to come, if that's quite all
right, please. Do you mind waiting a moment while I get
some money?"

"Okeydoke," said the reporter.

They said good-bye to the reporter at the gate of a small
farmyard, then bought two Aylesbury ducklings for seven
and sixpence each, arranged to collect them the evening

before Paul's birthday and walked home to find the local constable waiting in the nursery with a notebook and pencil in his hand. He was a big cheerful, red-faced man, and wanted to know exactly what had happened from beginning to end. Lucien told the story once more and the policeman took notes. Then Lottie, who appeared to have temporarily lost her usual fear of policemen, suggested that he might like to see some of the animals, and he said that was a delightful idea. With a wink at the others, she took him round the property and, at each step, she became more reckless. She told him that they took the ferrets poaching, that Cockade had bitten a chief constable—which was true—and that Dandylion often escaped from the orchard and trespassed and ate the vegetables in neighbours' gardens—which was only partly true. She put Tick and Tock up his sleeves and gave him some gooseberries.

Sheila, meanwhile, went back to her typewriting, while Jennet sat on a tree and grumbled to Lucien.

"Why can't we have a party to celebrate?" she asked. "It's so feeble—just going on as usual. We never seem to do anything gay nowadays."

"Who do you want to ask? There are no nice children round here as far as I can see—at least, except for your school friends, and you say the nicest has gone abroad."

"You wouldn't like the other one anyway. Haven't you and Marie any friends?"

"Of course we have and you know perfectly well that most of them live miles away. There's David Colman; he normally lives in London; at the moment I believe he's in Switzerland, trying to get some ski-ing around Zermatt. There's Dashwood; he's living just outside Ascot, if you know where that is, and Peter Arlingham-Drake, who comes from Porlock, and Alex, who's probably living with his grandmother in Fort William, which is in the wilds of Scotland. He's coming to stay in August, by the way, if Tibbles doesn't mind."

"What about Raymond?"

"I don't call him a friend; but for goodness' sake ask him, if you want him—only don't mention last night, whatever you do."

Jennet ran off and Lucien fetched a hammer and nails

and started to mend the garden fence. He wanted the place to be tidy for his father's return. Marie was sowing seeds in her garden. Charles had begun to get tea and was playing his mouth organ while he worked. Lottie was still showing the policeman round. Suddenly Lucien heard Sheila give a moan of despair and, after running across the orchard to where she sat beneath an apple tree, he found that the typewriter would not type any more. The ribbon would not wind properly and two of the letters were stuck.

"What shall we do? How can I ever finish *In Search of Love*? Frankie will be furious; and a bird has dropped something on one of Tibbles' pages!" wailed Sheila.

Lucien tried hard to mend the typewriter, but the Pennyfields had never been mechanically minded and he tried in vain. Presently he saw Lottie and the constable approaching The constable was all smiles.

"Well, what a jolly collection of animals you have got," he said. "Your sister Lottie says I can bring my little girl up to see your donkey and guinea fowl; she'll be that pleased—never seen a live donkey before—surprising how few there are about these parts."

"Oh good, I'm so glad. She must have a ride on Dandylion, if she would like one," said Lucien.

"What's up—gone and broken?" asked the constable looking at the typewriter.

"That's right," said Lucien.

"What do you think is wrong? The ribbon won't work. Do you understand typewriters at all?" Sheila asked hopefully.

"Can't say I do, but I'll have a look if you like."

"Oh, thank you, yes, please," said Sheila gratefully.

Then, to Lucien's horror, the constable started to take the typewriter to pieces. He unscrewed all the screws he could find and banged various parts which he thought were crooked; he demanded a screwdriver and a drop of oil and then, in the middle of his operations, Charles yelled that it was tea and Sheila invited him to come indoors and revive himself with a cup. He hesitated and then accepted. He did not stay long after that—just threw back three cups of tea, as though they were glasses of beer, made a few jovial remarks to Tibbles, ate a slice of cake and suddenly exclaimed at the lateness of the hour. At a quarter to five, after thanking everybody for a pleasant afternoon, he left—apparently forgetting the typewriter.

"Oh dear," said Sheila. "What will Daddy say when he finds it's broken?"

"It's a catastrophe," said Lottie.

"I've invited Raymond to a bonfire celebration supper with cider and baked potatoes," said Jennet.

"Oh, you *haven't*!" cried Marie in horror.

"Yes, I have. No one else would do anything about being gay."

"I shall hide," said Charles firmly.

"Oh, don't be a beast," said Lottie.

"Why shouldn't Jennet invite someone?" asked Sheila.

"No reason why she shouldn't," said Lucien. "Did you tell him what we were celebrating?"

"I said it was partly Daddy's return—or rather in anticipation of it," Jennet replied.

"Gosh, and he accepted! Did you say it was you personally who wanted him?" asked Marie.

"No, of course not."

"Did you say it was Lucien?"

"Not exactly."

"Oh!" exclaimed Marie.

"Don't be so jolly patronising," cried Jennet, picking up a bun and throwing it at Marie's face; it missed, hit the wall, fell on the floor and was quickly eaten by Brockie.

"Children, children! What are you thinking of! Now, Marie, don't threaten your younger sister. Never fight a person younger or smaller than yourself. What would your poor father say if he was here? Jennet, you ought to be ashamed of yourself, that you ought—behaving like a 'ooligan," said Tibbles.

"There's no need for Marie to be so beastly. Why shouldn't I have a party if I want one?"

"I think it's a lovely idea, but how are you getting the cider?" asked Sheila.

"Tibbles is going to arrange that, aren't you?" replied Jennet.

"Well, if you behave properly and don't start throwing
132

buns about. I've asked the boy what works for Bennet now to pop up to the public house and get a couple of quarts, but you younger ones are not to have more than half a glass each," said Tibbles.

"Oh, it's going to be marvellous. You are kind. Thank you so much," cried Lottie.

"Bang on—pretty hot," remarked Charles, mimicking the reporter's voice.

"Listen, twins," said Tibbles, "you've got to come in to bed at nine o'clock sharp, see, no later. Now run along anl make your bonfire. I'll do the washing up."

"You'll join in the party, too, won't you?" asked Jennet.

"I dare say."

While the younger Pennyfields started to build a bonfire, Lucien, Marie and Sheila tried to put the typewriter together again, but without success.

"I don't understand how it works at all," said Lucien.

The three of them stood and looked at all the different bits and pieces spread out before them on the table.

"Enough to make one go mad," remarked Lucien.

"Oh dear, Frankie will be cross."

"If she's anything like the heroine in *In Search of Love*, she will forgive us all," said Marie.

"And if she's anything like the villain, she'll shoot us," said Lucien, laughing.

"It's not funny," said Sheila. "I shall never get the book finished. It's all very well for you, you haven't tried to type it day after day, hour after hour." Her voice trembled, her eyes filled with tears. Then she cried, "Oh look!" And they saw, following her pointing finger, that a cat had walked with wet feet on one of the pages.

"Oh gosh!" exclaimed Marie.

"I shall *never* get it finished. Oh dear, what shall I do? What shall I do?" wailed Sheila.

"Don't start crying, for goodness' sake. We'll think of something," said Lucien.

"But it's getting so late. I go back to school in a week," said Sheila, her eyes filling with tears again.

Lucien felt in despair. "We'll have to take the typewriter into Kingham," he said.

133

"Shops take weeks to mend them," said Marie gloomily.

They stood then, just staring, with no idea what to do. The sound of a gate clicking wakened them from their reverie. It was Paul and the "lady in tweeds."

"Hallo, what's up?" asked Paul.

Marie explained, telling him about the policeman and the cat's paws. When she had finished, before Paul could speak, the "lady in tweeds" said, "There's no need to worry any more. I'll mend it. I understand typewriters. Long, long ago, when I was young and pretty, I was somebody's secretary and I used to have a typewriter just like this one."

She pulled the chair up to the table in a very business-like manner, sat down and started to work. She put it together again, oiled it, altered the position of the spools and then said, "Now, where's this dirty page?"

Sheila handed it to her and she started to type and once she had started she would not stop. "Years since I have done this," she said.

By half-past six, when she decided to leave, she had typed sixteen pages. The children were delighted, but she would not listen to their thanks.

When the "lady in tweeds" had gone, Paul said, "That was my last sitting and do you know what she has given me? She says it's a birthday present—two little ducklings. Come and look, they're in a box in the drive—or rather in a smart *hamper*, which she has given me too. One's a duck and the other a drake. I haven't decided what to call them. She says before we go back to school we are all to go and have tea with her and see the picture."

"How very kind," said Sheila.

"Are they Aylesburys?" asked Lucien.

"Yes," answered Paul.

Chapter Eighteen

CONTRARY to the Pennyfields' expectations, the bonfire party proved a success. Lucien invited Jimmy Dale, the boy who had brought the cider, to join in the celebrations and he was very gay indeed. Raymond produced a pocketful of fireworks, much to the delight of Lottie and Charles. Jennet played the gramophone and insisted on every one, including Tibbles, whom she adroitly captured, dancing round the bonfire; and Marie and Sheila surprised their brothers and sisters by suddenly carrying on to the scene an enormous fruit cake which Raymond and Jimmy said was delicious. Raymond did not boast as much as usual, because he was so full of the burglary; he explained at great length how he imagined the thieves had entered Upper Titwood Place and assured Lucien several times that the silver and jewellery were worth close on two hundred pounds. "The police were pretty smart catching them so soon; the bloke who was driving the car said the two cases were full of books, you know, but the bobby had had quite a different story by telephone, so he opened them and removing two layers of books found Mother's necklace and the silver from her dressing-table—just luck that we happened to be in town that night—staying at the *Dorchester*, you know—been there?—ought to try it, we had some wizard Curaçao," he said.

The Pennyfields were rather silent and this pleased Raymond, who, being fond of talking himself, liked a good listener. He expatiated on the burglary for nearly an hour and then Lottie fetched some of the animals, because she said they ought to join in the fun and he asked the Pennyfields why they bothered to keep a donkey. They were horrified and Jennet accused him of insulting Dandylion; and then he said he hadn't meant to cause offence, but surely it would be better to have a pony or horse. Marie said sharply that they couldn't afford one and chucked him a baked potato.

The two bottles of cider had not gone very far, although the younger Pennyfields had only been allowed half a glass each, and Lucien asked Jimmy, who was eighteen, if he could get them some more. Immediately Raymond said, "Let it be on me this time," and thrust five shillings into Jimmy's hand. Lucien remonstrated and said that he was host, but with no avail; in the end it was Raymond's money which paid for the two additional quarts of cider. At a quarter to ten they saw a constable bicycling by and, following Lucien's suggestion, dashed out and, making a circle round him, sang "He's a jolly good fellow." The constable looked very surprised, but it was several moments before they noticed that he was not their friend. When they *did* realise their mistake every one, except Lucien and Raymond, ran back into the orchard giggling. Lucien and Raymond apologised profusely; they both explained that they thought it was the local man, who was a friend of theirs. The policeman took it as a joke luckily, and after asking if they thought it was Guy Fawkes' Night remounted his bicycle and pedalled away. Afterwards they let off the fireworks and then Jennet and Paul had to go to bed and presently Raymond and Jimmy decided that they ought to go home.

The next day Marie and Jennet rose very early to take the pig to market. It was a beautiful light morning with a little nip in the air. When they caught Dandylion they found that the hair on her legs was singed; she had been lying in the ashes of the bonfire; they giggled a great deal over this and wakened Lottie, who came running out barefooted and helped them start. Solomon accompanied them. As they jogged along the road the sky grew lighter, until they knew that it was blue and then, in the east, there crept a rosy hue. The cocks ceased crowing; the cows in the small, sheltered meadows waited patiently to be taken in and milked; the dew still sparkled on the hedges; rabbits darted still amongst the wet grass.

Marie whistled and Jennet sang and Dandylion's cart made a pleasant rattling sound. They arrived at the farm at five minutes past six. At first they thought nobody was up and about; then they found a labourer, who said Mr. Hayes, the farmer, was still in bed.

"I reckon 'e didn't expect you so early like," said the labourer, "thought you 'ad something a bit bigger—horse and cart, I shouldn't wonder. Still, I know what pig it be —fine sow, she is. Bring your little cart round this way. We'll get it close to the sty if we can."

There followed the usual screaming as the pig was pushed into the cart by the labourer and Marie. Eventually she was firmly installed with her legs tied together and covered by a large net, which the children were told must be returned to the farm as soon as possible. When they left, it was twenty minutes past six. Kingham market was seven miles away and they were proposing to walk leading the donkey. Although they had each eaten a bowl of the despised cereal before leaving, they were beginning to feel hungry.

"Never mind," said Marie cheerfully. "I've got my pocket half-crown with me, so we can buy some hot rolls in the suburbs—that is, if we are as lucky as Paul and they don't mention 'BUs.'"

After this suggestion they did not speak much, because the sow kept them busy. She screamed and several times tried to escape from underneath her net. One furious housewife came running to her gate in her dressing-gown, thinking that the children were making the noise. She started to lecture them as she came down the path, saying that they were a disgrace, waking every one up at such an hour—that they ought to be in a home. When she saw that it was a pig, she apologised and Jennet broke down with an awful attack of giggles. Dandylion did not think the journey at all funny; her step became slower and slower the nearer she came to Kingham. Eventually Jennet tried riding her, sitting on top of the pad which was rather uncomfortable. This was much more successful and Marie had to run to keep up. They stopped at the first open baker's shop that they saw, but the girl behind the counter would not let them have any bread, because they had no BUs.

Accordingly, when they noticed a placard farther up the road saying, *Pip's Café. Breakfasts, Luncheons, Teas, Dinner, Snacks*, they decided to treat themselves to a proper breakfast. Jennet felt quite excited; she was very hungry and it was a long time since she had eaten a meal out. Dandylion was glad to stop and, after fixing the net more firmly, they tied her to a convenient lamp-post and went into the café. The outside had looked sordid, but the inside was very bright and clean; there were about a dozen red enamel-topped tables, a smart red counter and a pay desk. The walls were cream, the woodwork red and the ceiling white. An electric clock said that the time was ten minutes past eight.

"No need to hurry," sighed Marie, sitting down at a table. The café was empty.

"I wonder whether we ought to go to the counter and ring a bell or something," said Jennet.

"I'll tap the table with my half-crown," Marie told her.

They tapped and they talked in loud voices, and presently a young woman appeared on the scene and they explained that they wanted breakfast.

"It's scrambled eggs," she told them, disappearing again.

"This is fun. I do love eating out," said Jennet.

"Sit down, Soloman, and don't water at the mouth. There's something to be said for not doing things often, it makes one enjoy them all the more really."

"Like going to the cinema. I'm sure we enjoy that much more than Raymond. Ah, here are the eggs. How lovely; thank you so much."

They were very hungry and though it was only dried eggs on toast, they declared them delicious. Soloman licked the plates, while the children started on the bread, butter and marmalade; they had not given the sow a thought. And suddenly they heard shouts and yells of laughter coming from outside.

"Gosh! The pig!" cried Marie, leaping to her feet.

In a moment they were on the pavement in time to see the fat white sow dash down a side street. After her they ran; the onlookers roared with laughter; little boys on their way to school whistled derisively. Dandylion brayed; Soloman barked. Marie, a fast runner, soon gained on the pig. Jennet was laughing so much that she could hardly run at all. She told Soloman to *head it*, and Soloman, mistaking her orders, nipped the pig's heels, causing her to run all the faster.

Marie was worried; she thought the farmer would be rightly furious if their charge was killed by a car or died of heart failure; he would probably sue them for negligence—or rather their father, as they were minors—and who could blame him? A moment later she passed the pig and tried to drive her back to Jennet, who was still laugh-

138

ing. Soloman spoiled everything; he was very excited now, and with a bark of delight, drove the pig into a garden where, as luck would have it, the borders were littered with glass cloches. If only the pig had been wearing a collar it would have been much easier, but, as things were, Marie could find nothing of which to catch hold; and Soloman made matters worse. Jennet stopped laughing when she saw the formidable rows of cloches and suggested ways of cornering their charge. First they tried to drive her into a little toolshed, but she slipped past them; then they tried to get her against a hedge, but again in vain. Jennet managed to grab a foreleg during this attempt, only to release her hold when she received a spirited kick in the face a few minutes later.

"This is terrible. We've got to catch her. We'll be late for market," cried Marie.

"Soloman, *will* you come here," called Jennet, as the collie started to nip the pig's heels once more.

"If we don't capture her soon she'll die of heart failure, I'm sure she will," said Marie dismally.

"Get her round the neck next time," said Jennet.

"Quick," yelled Marie, "she's going up the garden path; we can get her in the porch. Run round to the left or she'll slip past the window to the back of the house."

Jennet did as she was bid, and the next minute the pig was across the doorstep and in the porch. At last, thought Marie, stretching out her arms; but as the pig entered the porch, the owner of the house opened the front door and, instead of grabbing the sow's hind legs, Marie's hands clutched at thin air, and the pig bolted through the hall and through a dark brown doorway.

"What is happening?" asked the owner of the house.

Marie did not wait to answer, crying, "Sorry," she dashed after the pig, into the kitchen and round the table.

Jennet, meanwhile, was overcome by a fresh set of giggles; powerless, she leaned against the porch, clasping her sides. Suddenly the owner of the house, an agreeable-looking, middle-aged woman, began to giggle too; shaking with laughter, she went to help Marie, who by this time had caught the pig and was tying its two fore and two hind trotters together with some string she had seized from the kitchen table.

"I'm most terribly sorry," said Marie.

"My dear," spluttered the middle-aged woman, "it's quite the funniest thing I've ever seen happen in my life. A pig! And what a big one! I wouldn't mind a nice bit of bacon off that, no, I wouldn't." At this thought she burst into peals of laughter. "My husband was grumbling this morning, said he never had a decent breakfast nowadays. Oh, how I wish he had seen this piggy! How he would have laughed!" she continued, when she had regained her self-control.

"She's too good for bacon—a jolly sporting pig," said Jennet, coming into the kitchen.

"We're going to be late," hissed Marie. "We'll have to carry her," she added, and then, to the agreeable-looking, middle-aged woman, "Good-bye, and thank you very much for being so nice about everything."

They ran down the path to the road, but when they got through the gate they had to rest—the pig was so heavy.

"I can't think how she managed to get her feet untied before or the net off," said Marie.

"I bet some of those boys which were hanging around let her go as a joke," panted Jennet; "they all carry knives."

"Wretches."

It took the children a quarter of an hour to take the pig back to Dandylion and ten minutes to fix her firmly in the cart. The time was ten to nine when they eventually paid for their breakfast and started again for the market.

"Thank goodness we set off so early. Selling doesn't begin till half-past," said Marie.

"Oh, it *was* funny, though!" said Jennet.

The sun was shining when they reached the market. The nearby shops were gay with spring frocks. Dandylion brayed and every one seemed to laugh and Marie felt the happiness she had experienced in the early morning return to her. It was wonderful just to put one foot in front of the other and to feel the sun warming one's back and to see the sky, so blue behind the chimney-pots.

"We've got here," said Jennet, and, as she spoke, she felt a great sense of achievement.

Chapter Nineteen

"YOUR poor father's telephoned. He's spent the night in London and will be home for lunch to-day, so run in quick and make your beds and shut your drawers and tidy yourselves up." These words, spoken by Tibbles, greeted Marie and Jennet's return. Indoors, Lottie and Charles were cleaning silver. Butt was scrubbing the dining-room floor. Sheila was arranging daffodils in an enormous blue jug and Paul was dreamily polishing a French mahogany table.

"Have you heard?" cried Lottie. ". . . Yes? Oh, Jennet, do come and help. I'm sure Charles and I are never going to get finished in time and I *do* want to brush the dogs, and you might start the gramophone, please—every one is so gloomy."

"Now, don't come a-walking in 'ere with your muddy shoes," said Butt.

"Did you eat something hot for breakfast before you left?" asked Tibbles, who had followed them.

"Well . . ." hesitated Marie.

"Does that mean you *didn't*?" interrupted Tibbles. "After all I told Lucien, too! Now, go into the larder, fetch out that nice little tin with the lady on it and 'ave some biscuits and butter and hot milk. You can take a couple of eggs too, if you like."

"We did manage to stop at a café," said Marie.

"Please, need we have *hot* milk? I *do* hate it so," asked Jennet.

"Now 'urry along and do as you're told. I haven't time to help you this morning—got your poor father's room to finish."

"No good arguing or explaining. We'll have cold milk—she won't really mind; it's not as though we're wet or anything," said Marie.

141

They took off their shoes and, jumping the wetter bricks in the dining-room, reached the larder.

A few minutes later Lucien returned carrying a large tin of white paint.

"I hope nobody minds me buying this. But I thought we had better paint the drive gate; it looks so awfully dingy," he said.

They were all busy then. Marie helped peel vegetables; Jennet assisted the twins, who were determined to clean out the ferrets' hutch and the mice's cage, and to brush Dandylion and the dogs.

Tibbles said their poor father would be hungry and cooked Sunday's leg of mutton; she had managed to buy some new potatoes and she made both onion and mint sauce, because she could not remember which he liked best. At twelve o'clock she sent the children upstairs to wash their faces and "try to make themselves respectable."

Paul thought all the fuss silly. Surely their own father ought to see them as they really were? And what did clothes matter anyway? Lucien thought that the most annoying part about it was that now they could no longer tidy up the property, for fear of becoming dirty. Lottie tried to remember what their father looked like and wondered whether he would bring them any presents. They waited in the nursery. Charles soon became completely absorbed in a book called *Brave Buccaneers*. Sheila wondered whether her father would really like a leg of mutton on such a hot day, and mended an ankle sock.

Half-past twelve came and then a quarter to one.

"I'm going outside," said Paul, "to see my ducklings."

"Lucien, Lucien!" called Tibbles, "we've finished the salt and I've never noticed. Run down and get me some more from Bullits, please."

"Oh, goodness" exclaimed Sheila, putting down the sock and jumping to her feet, "I've left the typewriter and *In Search of Love* out in the garden and I don't want the cats over everything again."

As she walked through the door, Paul came running in yelling, "Quick! Good news, good news."

"Has Daddy arrived?" asked Sheila, checking her step.

"No, Minnie's decided to celebrate—she's had kittens—ten tabbies."

A moment later Tibbles and all the Pennyfield children, except Lucien, were in the granary and it was there that Patrick Pennyfield, guided by the twins' loud voices, found them.

"Hallo . . . Kittens? What a crowd of people!" he said, standing with a bemused expression. It felt strange to be back at Scholar Farm after nearly a year's absence and to think that he possessed such a large family! No wonder Guy Woodford thought him calm; you needed to be calm if you were responsible for seven children, thought Patrick Pennyfield. And then every one started talking.

"You *must* come and see the animals. You've never met Tick and Tock," cried Lottie, tugging him by the sleeve.

"Did you 'ave a good journey? Lunch is ready when you want it, sir," said Tibbles.

"Were you seasick?" asked Charles.

"You look tired, Daddy. Was the train very crowded? Don't talk so loudly, twins," said Sheila.

"How do you do, Tibbles? No, I wasn't sick. Lottie, this is my only decent London suit."

"Oh dear, you've got some white from the gate on it too. Lucien forgot to put up the notice, I suppose. Luckily we've got a bottle of turps," said Marie.

"Here's Cockade. Arrr, look—she's pleased to see you, she's wagging her tail—arr, faithful Cockade. Do you know she killed some rats and that beast Janet tried to bite her vein—you know, the important one," said Lottie.

"She nearly bled to death," added Charles.

"Hallo," said Lucien, walking up from behind, a tin of salt in his hand. "How nice to see you back. Are you very hungry or did you have a good breakfast? Can I take those cases in for you?"

A look of relief passed across Patrick Pennyfield's face.

"Ah, hallo, Lucien. My hotel provided me with an excellent breakfast, thank you. If you would take the small case, I can manage the other two. I feel quite lost, can hardly remember the names of my own children; you'll have to help me to tell them all apart, please. Yes, Lottie, I would love to see Clip and Clop—in a moment—no, not now. Oh, sorry—*Tick* and *Tock*. You should speak more distinctly. Good girl, Cockade. Hallo, Brockie— steady—London trousers—*down*. Good dog, Soloman."

They started walking to the house.

"I'm going to play a gramophone record to celebrate. What would you like, Daddy?" asked Jennet.

"What a question—anything, except 'Oogie Boogie' or 'Rule Britannia.' "

"Say one."

"Go and put on the 'Merry Widow' and stop bothering your poor father; he's tired. Sheila, can you help me with the dishing up, please?" said Tibbles.

At lunch Paul said, "I've knocked about a bit lately. The other day I spent the night in Ealing and ate breakfast with a pawnbroker and his wife."

Tibbles looked upset and Marie kicked Paul under the table.

Then Marie told him about their morning adventures and about all the Scholar Farm Services, but did not mention the two night expeditions. Their father laughed a good deal, especially when he heard Lucien was coaching Timothy. By the time Marie had finished and Patrick Pennyfield had told them about some of his adventures, it was half-past two and he went upstairs to unpack, while the children and Tibbles washed up and fed the animals. Then came the present-opening. He had remembered everybody, even Butt—although she would not be given hers until the next morning. Lottie was the first to tear away the wrapping, and she cried, "Look, look, a scarf— how lovely. Thank you so much, thanks awfully."

It was a red hand-woven one, found by Patrick Pennyfield in Paris, in a stall in the rue Sebastopol. Jennet was the next to display her present—a white china horse, bought in Montmartre; she christened him Picasso at once.

The others all opened their presents at the same moment. Tibbles' was the largest and the most expensive —a cuckoo clock, which fascinated the children from the first. Sheila's present was a scarf, a blue silk one, bought in a more respectable quarter than Lottie's. Lucien's present was a book on the works of Toulouse Lautrec, which

144

Patrick Pennyfield had seen in a shop window in the Avenue de l'Opera. Paul's was a slim, black fountain pen, bought in despair, and Marie's a little oil painting by a completely unknown artist, of an obscure part of Paris. Charles's was a large knife with two blades, a corkscrew and a screwdriver.

All the children were very pleased. Lucien started to read his book and was soon in need of a French dictionary. Paul christened his pen Matthew after the poet, Matthew Arnold; and then, being reminded that the pen was of French nationality, rechristened it Victor Hugo. Charles tried in vain to think of a name for his knife, while Lottie tied her scarf round her waist like a sash and proclaimed herself a pirate. Sheila put hers round her neck and went upstairs to look at herself in a mirror. Marie and Patrick Pennyfield hung Marie's picture in her bedroom and Tibbles started to try to put her clock together and wondered where her employer had bought it.

It was four o'clock when at last Lottie managed to drag her father to see the animals and then, after all the trouble the expedition was not very successful, because Dandylion kicked him on the shin and Magpie scratched him on the hand and Janet tried to bite his finger; but at the end, when he had finished looking at the tortoises, Jennet managed to ask a question which she had been meaning to ask for the last month; she had not told the others of her intention, because she thought they might disapprove.

"Daddy," she said, "can we have some ponies, please?"

There was an awful silence, broken by Marie saying, "Shut up."

Then Patrick Pennyfield said, "Well, it's very difficult. Ponies eat an awful lot. I expect I could afford to buy you one, but who should I buy it for? Seven people can't all ride the same pony. By right, I suppose if I *did* get one, it should be for Lucien and that would mean a horse of about 15.2, which would be hopeless for any of you smaller people; then Lucien is away at school most of the time, so he wouldn't make full use of it." He sat down on the fallen apple tree and Cockade immediately jumped on to his knee and covered his face with kisses.

"It doesn't matter," said Sheila quickly, "We don't need
145

ponies; we can easily wait until we are earning our livings and then buy ourselves one."

"Dandylion might be jealous, too," remarked Lottie, trying to be tactful.

"We'll see. I want to take you all for a holiday abroad some time. You can't possibly grow up without having ventured out of England. I don't know where we'll go—probably Paris for a day or two. Switzerland is too expensive."

"But what about all the animals? We can't leave them," asked Lottie.

"We can easily fix them up," said Lucien.

"Somebody like Mrs. Butland can caretake and look after them," said Patrick Pennyfield.

As he spoke, Tibbles called Sheila to come indoors; she hurried away. Lottie guessed she was going to make a cake for tea.

"I'm going to call my knife Louis, because he's king of knives," declarel Charles.

"Somebody's mended the garden fence, I see," said Patrick Pennyfield, removing Cockade gently, rising and walking across the orchard to look at Lucien's work.

Marie turned on Jennet. "You shouldn't ask for things. You know Daddy can't afford to buy us ponies. Why do you think he's only got one London suit? Why do you think he sold the mahogany bookcase last year for a hundred pounds? Most families of seven haven't got nearly so many things as we have. I believe my school fees are about sixty pounds a term. Anyhow, you know we are trying to earn enough money to try and buy and keep ponies ourselves. You don't think he likes us having less than other children, do you?" asked Marie.

Jennet was saved an answer because, as her sister finished speaking, Sheila came running out of the house looking frantic with worry.

"Oh, Marie," she cried, "something awful has happened—all my work and all the work of the 'lady in tweeds'—it's finished—Spookies been sick on it. What am I to do? I go back to school in four days' time. Frankie White will be so cross—twenty pages all ruined, *ruined*." She threw herself down on the grass.

"Oh gosh! I don't know," said Marie helplessly.

"What is the matter, Sheila? Have you got appendicitis?" asked Patrick Pennyfield, coming back.

"It's *In Search of Love*," said Marie.

"Who's in search of love?—you can't be at your age," said Patrick Pennyfield.

"It's a book," said Marie.

"Oh, well," said Patrick Pennyfield, in consoling accents, "I shouldn't take any notice of it—authors are often very misled people. Who's it by, anyway?"

"Frankie White."

"Never heard of her, but she sounds unconvincing. I supposed it's published by someone like Febbs."

"It isn't published."

"All the more reason to take no notice of it then. Come on, Sheila, don't be silly; hop up. Miss Frankie White probably doesn't know what she's talking about. Now, if it was *Jane Eyre* or *Wuthering Heights*, I could understand. My sister—Aunt Louisa—she always used to cry over them. She used to lock herself in her bedroom when she reached the piece where Jane leaves Mr. Rochester. Have you read them? I'm sure you would like them much better than—what is it?—*In Search of Love*."

"You don't know what I'm talking about. It's some typing I'm trying to do and Spookie's been sick over it, which is so mean of her, because I've tried to type it so many times. I wanted to earn some money," said Sheila, rising to her feet.

"Who on earth is *Spookie*, another mouse, a guinea pig, or what?"

"Gosh! of course you haven't seen her; she's mine. I bought her from a simply horrid pet shop for half a crown. I'm sure she didn't mean to spoil *In Search of Love*; she probably thought it was newspaper. Come on, you must come and look at her, please," said Jennet.

They walked through the garden to the house and Marie explained about Miss Frankie White's novel and Patrick Pennyfield said, "Never mind, Sheila; I'll help you with it to-morrow. I haven't typed for years, but I expect we'll manage. Now look, as a special treat, you younger children can all stay up to dinner to-night. I've brought two bottles of claret and a couple of chickens, which are probably on the tough side. Sheila, you seem to understand the household affairs, can you find claret glasses for six and liqueur glasses for Jennet and the twins?—we don't want them tipsy."

"Oh, can't *we* have claret glasses?" asked Jennet. "I'm sure I've got a wonderful head."

"I'm arranging this dinner, not you, and I'm sure you haven't. Where is this Spookie? Don't let her be sick on me," said Patrick Pennyfield.

Chapter Twenty

SHEILA thought that the next day was the happiest of her life; she wakened to hear the birds singing in the tall beeches by the garden gate and saw, through her window, a sapphire sky and sunshine lying golden on the sparkling lawn and just a branch of cherry blossom peeping round the corner of the house; she wakened with a light heart and a feeling that to-day nothing could go wrong, and, springing out of bed, she ran barefoot down the stairs and made her father, Tibbles, Lucien and Marie cups of tea, which she took up to them on a tray.

And the especially marvellous thing about that morning was that everybody else seemed to waken as happily. Even Butt came singing to her work, with no tragedy to relate. And there were enough eggs in the larder for each person to have one boiled for breakfast. And, as it was Saturday, the *Kingham Star* came and on page two there was a large column and a half headed with:

"MOTHERLESS TALENTED CHILDREN LOSE DUCKS.
AID POLICE CATCH THIEF."

And starting:

"On Wednesday night Lucien, Sheila, Marie and Paul
148

Pennyfield determined to avenge the loss of two ducks. . . ."

There followed a short description of their experiences on Wednesday night, keeping to the gist of Lucien's story and then a few lines describing all the Pennyfield children, and Tibbles, and her remarks about their accomplishments.

It finished:

"These thieves have to answer not only for the jewels and silver—valued at £250—but for scores of chickens, which have been disappearing from farms and small-holdings in the Kingham district during the past two months. . . ."

And there was the photograph that Sheila had given to the reporter, looking very smudgy.

The children and Tibbles were very excited and, of course, Patrick Pennyfield was extremely surprised.

"You deceitful people, not telling me a word about it," he laughed, and then he read out loud a description of Tibbles, which he thought especially funny: . . ."a tall, formidable woman, reminiscent of the Victorian era, with a kindly smile, who is obviously very proud of her seven charges."

"I like the description of you, too, Jennet—*lively, bespectacled and modest*—about the first person who has ever described you as modest, isn't it? But tell me, who is this man for whom those *wild, attractive* twins weeded? And did you really have breakfast with a pawnbroker and his wife, Paul? In *Ealing*—it sounds fantastic."

Marie and Paul explained and enlarged the story. When they had finished, Lucien said, "It seems ridiculous, doesn't it? We did so little really; it was all luck—being at the right place at the right moment. It's not as though we made careful plans; we did everything in such a haphazard fashion. I don't think we deserve all this fuss and to-do. Talented children indeed!"

"That was Tibbles' doing," said Marie.

"Well, I 'ad to say something, didn't I? And I only told the truth."

"Quite right," said Patrick Pennyfield; and then the telephone started to ring and for the next twenty minutes it rang at regular intervals. The Pennyfields had no idea that they possessed so many acquaintances. "The lady in tweeds" was the first to congratulate them and Mrs. Phillips was the second. The last and the most important was Mrs. George, Raymond's mother; she was important, because she made what the Pennyfields considered to be a very kind and very exciting suggestion; she started by saying how grateful she was to them for helping the police to retrieve her necklace, which was of great sentimental value, and two brooches and, as she was a nervous, affected and talkative woman, this took a considerable time; in fact, Marie was becoming impatient when Mrs. George eventually made her proposition.

"Raymond tells me that you all *adore* riding," said Mrs. George. "Well, my dear, we have two horses—don't ask me whether they are good or bad horses, because I simply don't *know*; isn't it dreadful? I can't tell one end from another; I really can't. I don't know our two apart—don't laugh, it's the truth. Well, my dear, to get back to what I was saying, they *are* horses and I *do* know that dear Raymond doesn't give them enough exercise. He does so many other exciting things that he doesn't really have time; he just likes to take them hunting once or twice a season and that's all—can't bear hacking, my dear. Do you know what he said the other day?—don't laugh—'Mother,' he said, 'this is not the eighteenth or even the nineteenth century. This is a mechanised age; I move by and with mechanism'—just like that. I haven't suggested that he should take the horses out since. Still, there you are. Well, my dear, what I'm trying to say is, would you and your brothers and sisters like to exercise them? Now, think carefully. Don't say *yes* if you don't mean it."

"We would love to. I can promise you that without thinking at all. It's a wonderful offer, thank you very much," said Marie, longing to fling down the receiver and tell her brothers and sisters the good news.

"There now! I told Raymond you would be pleased to do it and he said Lucien was one of those *clever* chaps and wouldn't want to hack a couple of old nags about the countryside. Aren't boys silly sometimes? Dear Raymond was quite cross with me ringing up at all. Now, let me see, if you come over this afternoon you'll be able to talk to Mr. Ray; he's the dear old man who comes twice a week to help Bert and Mr. Todd with the garden and he knows all about horses. My dear, he's got quite the bandiest legs you've ever seen and he simply *adores* Raymond."

"That's marvellous," said Marie, "thank you so much. We would love to come this afternoon and talk everything over. We don't ride very well, by the way. Lucien's the best; he had some lessons when he was seven and last summer he stayed with a friend at Ascot and rode every day for a fortnight. An aunt gave me a course of lessons the term before last—there's riding at my school—but that's all I've done, apart from sitting on Dandylion occasionally, and the others have only had a few odd rides."

"Well, my dear, come along at half-past two and you'll find old Mr. Ray pottering about the stables and he'll tell you all there is to tell."

"Thank you; we certainly will. Good-bye." Marie rang off and ran through into the dining-room, where she found her father, Sheila and Lucien struggling with the typewriter.

She called the rest of the family and told them about Mrs. George's suggestion, which sent all the younger members into ecstasies; until Lucien pointed out that the horses might be much too tall for the twins to ride and then Lottie and Charles became lost in gloom. Jennet fetched the gramophone and played "I've Got Sixpence," "Roll Out the Barrel," "Keep Right On to the End of the Road" and "Tipperary," which her father said sounded frightful at this time in the morning and were inappropriate for the occasion. Sheila continued struggling with the typewriter. Lucien ran upstairs to see if his breeches still fitted. Marie found and started to read *A Horse to Ride*, by Colonel Ribb, which was the only instructive book on horsemanship the Pennyfields possessed. Paul went to look at his ducklings and the twins sat on the window ledge and wished that they were taller.

At ten o'clock Sheila and Patrick Pennyfield finished mending the typewriter and started to type *In Search of*

151

Love—or rather Patrick Pennyfield started to type and Sheila watched and handed him new pages and the rubber, which was in constant use, because Patrick Pennyfield thought some of the characters, who were meant to be serious, extremely funny and, every now and then, he had to stop to laugh, and before he stopped he always made a mistake—pressed FIG instead of CAP or put the letters of a word down in the wrong order.

By lunch time he had only typed six pages and Sheila's hopes were waning. Lucien had promised to help her during the evening, but, as *In Search of Love* promised to be at least two hundred and fifty pages, his offer did not cheer her very much. While they ate, the children talked mostly of Raymond's horses. Lucien said they were called Bruno and Juno, and he thought Juno was really a pony of about 14.2 Then the twins started to shriek that if she was a pony they could ride her, and Patrick Pennyfield noticed that his children's table manners were not all that could be desired.

"Lottie," he said, "don't talk with your mouth full. Charles, sit up properly; you look like a sack of potatoes. You needn't eat quite so fast, Marie; nobody's coming to snatch your lunch away and Jennet, you *must* come into Kingham with me to-morrow and get some new spectacles —those look perfectly frightful."

"To-morrow's Sunday," said Jennet, "so the shops will be shut."

"Well, on Monday then."

"Oh no," shrieked Lottie. "It's Paul's birthday and we must ride on his birthday."

"Don't shriek, Lottie, and for goodness' sake stop tilting your chair and behaving like a jack-in-the-box. You can't all go riding and you can't ride from dawn to dark. Charles, are you holding a pistol or a spoon?"

"A spoon."

"Well, hold it properly."

"We wanted to celebrate," said Jennet.

"Oh, shut up," said Paul. "It's *my* birthday, and I'm sure there will be time for you to go into Kingham. I don't want to celebrate all day long; it would be most exhausting. Can I have some more treacle tart, please?"

152

"What's a jack-in-the-box?" asked Lottie.

"I've just been thinking," said Lucien suddenly. "We've still got ten pounds in the post office; we only drew two pounds out, didn't we? And according to our box upstairs the Scholar Farm earning campaign has four pounds fifteen shillings and sixpence to its credit—not much; but still, we've had some fun. I think, though, we ought to decide what to do with the money. Do we want to spend it, put it in the post office or what?"

"Spend it," said Jennet promptly.

"No," shrieked Lottie, "we are going to earn some more in the summer holidays. The circus will make lots. Dandylion hasn't learned to lie down, but she stands on a tub and shakes hands, and I can canter facing the tail. And, as for Tock, she pulls a miniature log about beautifully. If Lucien would make a cart, she could go in that, which would be much better. And, just think—*Minnie's kittens*; they would be wonderful. I'll teach them to stand in a row with their front feet on flower pots, as miniature tubs. And Charles is training Tick, aren't you, Charles? And now that the tortoises are waking up, we can plan an act for them. Honestly, we can have a simply marvellous circus. I can go on practising while you are at school. And what about the magazine? I've written lots of things for that, only Marie won't accept any of them—nor Jennet's *Story of Spookie* for that matter. I vote we put the money aside and then at the end of the summer holidays we begin to think about spending it." Lottie paused a moment to gain breath.

"There's Sheila's typing—that's going to bring in four pounds," said Charles.

"If it *ever* gets finished," said Sheila dismally.

"The magazine is really filling up quite well," Marie told the others. "We have three of Paul's poems, one article by Lottie on training mice, one article, one short story and one poem by Lucien—plus drawings—*The Art of Driving Donkeys* and *A Pony to Ride* by me, two useful recipes and an article on arranging flowers by Sheila. We have a poem on gaiety by Jennet. In fact Charles is the only really slack person."

153

"It's your fault; you refused *School Masters' Sins* and my poem about Tick," said Charles.

"Yes, I'm sorry, but we couldn't publish those digs at your headmaster—it was too obvious," explained Marie.

"Are you aware that it is now ten minutes to two?" asked Patrick Pennyfield, rising from the table.

"No," shrieked Lottie.

"I don't know what to wear," said Charles.

"You can wear my trousers when you ride; we can change behind a bush; only, put on your biggest pair of shorts or I shall be in the soup," said Paul.

"Oh dear, you look so *awful* in those trousers," said Sheila.

"Thank goodness my old jodhs still fit. Please, Tibbles, can we wash this up with tea?" asked Marie.

Chapter Twenty-one

As THEY reached the top of Titwood Hill and looked down into the valley the whole land seemed to be smiling; the winding silver river sparkled in the sunshine; the meadows and the trees made a carpet of greens; even the sad willows raised their heads a little in the breeze to glance upwards to the laughing fleecy clouds, that darted hither and thither in their world of blue.

Marie was riding Bruno and Paul was riding Juno; the rest of the Pennyfield children were walking.

"What a wonderful view," exclaimed Marie, halting the dark brown gelding. "I believe I've always been wrong. It is not what you *do* that matters. It is things like this view; it is beauty—sunshine on the meadows; a branch of cherry blossom against a blue spring sky; the touch of the breeze on your face; the sparkle of dew in the early morning; music and the carefree song of birds—oh, I don't know. I can't explain what I mean; but it's wonderful days like this that makes one feel happy; not the fact that you've earned five, ten, a thousand pounds. It's just to be able to be out, to enjoy it all—to see the beauty of it. Oh gosh, it's wonderful to be on a horse again, at last!"

"My turn now," said Sheila.

"And mine," shrieked Lottie.

They had drawn lots before they started to decide in what order they should ride. Sheila and Jennet were to be the last to have their turns. Lucien and Charles had been the first. It had been very complicated working everything out, until Lottie suggested that Marie should be allowed two turns, because she was going back to school three days before the other Pennyfields.

Now Lucien looked at his watch and said, "You're wrong; Marie and Paul have got five more minutes."

"Come on," said Marie, "don't let's stand still."

They rode down the bridle path towards the river, keeping to the same slow pace at which they had travelled all afternoon. Sheila walked beside Juno, just in case Paul should get into difficulties; but, so far, apart from not wishing to leave each other, the handsome brown gelding and the smaller, lighter brown mare had behaved excellently. They were both very unfit, having not been ridden since December, and felt no wish to hurry. Although Juno was 14.2 hands high, Charles had been completely at home on her and was already talking about trying a canter next time.

At the bottom of the hill they turned off on to a road and Sheila and Lottie took the horses.

"We are lucky," said Lucien, "being able to ride all the summer, but we must be careful not to spoil Bruno and Juno. I think we ought to spend some of our earnings on riding lessons."

"Jolly good idea! I'm feeling a bit unsafe now—steady Bruno," said Sheila.

"The Kingham Road Stables look fairly efficient," said Lucien, "and the four pounds fifteen shillings might go quite a long way. I think he wants a looser head, Sheila."

"But what about your gun?" asked Lottie.

"I'll wait until I've left school and am earning my living. I haven't much time to go shooting, especially if I'm going to split the holidays between making money and riding."

"Oh dear, we haven't got very near a hundred pounds, have we?" said Sheila.

"You wait. The circus will earn lots and lots," declared Lottie, running her hands through Juno's neatly pulled black mane.

"I shouldn't leave go of the reins," advised Sheila.

"You know, I don't think we really deserved to help catch that thief," mused Marie. "We really behaved most awfully badly—peeping in people's sheds and wandering around at night. It would have been frightful for Tibbles if we had been murdered; even if Daddy had not blamed her, she would have probably been haunted by remorse for life."

"Oh well, what's done's done," said Jennet.

"I told Lottie that man with the large nose was nasty, but she wouldn't agree; she said he was very agreeable," remarked Charles suddenly.

"I've always been a bad judge of character. . . . Dare you to canter next time," challenged Lottie.

"I'll see," replied Charles.

"You're afraid, I believe," said Lottie.

"I'm not."

And then they reached the back gate of Upper Titwood House, where Mr. Ray was awaiting their return. He was very pleased to hear that the children had enjoyed their ride and helped them turn out the horses and clean the tack.

It was half-past four when they eventually started for home, and they all felt hungry.

"We must ring up Mrs. George and tell her how we got on and thank her," said Lucien.

"Next time Charles and I can bring Dandylion and ride her, too," said Lottie.

As they walked back along the dark and twisty road, past little cottages, meadows grazed by sleepy cattle, small woods fresh and green with new limp leaves, they made plans for the future.

They also tried to remember some of the horrible things they had said about Raymond so that they might swallow their words. Charles said that he had declared him like a school marm, which must have been unjust because school marms didn't lend horses to children. Jennet recalled saying that he did not deserve to be rich and Lucien recalled

156

saying that he was stupid and not worth thinking about. When they reached the end of the lane, Jennet said:

"I know one thing—now we've got horses to ride, I'm not going ratting any more. I haven't driven the sight of those wretched corpses from my mind yet. I'm never going to kill another animal."

"Well, I know another thing," said Lucien, "we mustn't go wandering around at night in future. It's not fair on Tibbles and we are very lucky that she hasn't been really furious with us. It can't be much fun to be responsible for children, who do idiotic things like going off in strangers' cars and spending the night meandering around Ealing. I think Daddy's a little horrified by our past behaviour. One day, Jennet, you'll step into a murderer's car and have your throat cut."

"I think you're perfectly right, Lucien," said Sheila.

Paul said, "I've thought of the beginning of a poem about my ride to-day. Do you think it will be suitable for the magazine? It's this:

"Blue is the sky and white the laughing clouds
    Darting hither, thither in the breeze.
And lovely is the greenery that crowds
    To either side of me amid the trees.
And laughing is my heart, for now I ride
    Astride a horse—ah, dearest dream come true!
And happiness I feel with every single stride
    And greatest joy that ever yet I knew."

"Can hearts laugh, Paul?" asked Marie.

"Poetic licence," said Lucien. "I think it's jolly good, except for *every single stride*, which doesn't seem right somehow."

"Yes, I must alter that," mused Paul.

"Doesn't Scholar Farm look lovely in the sunshine?" said Sheila, "so white and clean and homely."

The children found their father painting the orchard gate.

"I though I would carry on Lucien's good work. Did you all fall off?" he inquired.

"Certainly not. The horses went jolly well and we had

157

a wonderful ride. Bruno's dark brown with a Roman nose and black points, upstanding but not hefty or cumbersome, and Juno's a lighter brown and also lighter in build, and she's got a sweet little star and a dish face," said Marie.

"I'm very glad, because I think I might be able to buy you a pony or horse or both, after all. Rather an interesting letter arrived by the lunch-time post. I'm getting a rise—quite a considerable rise—and if Jennet doesn't break 'her spectacles too often and you refrain from poaching and causing other unnecessary expenses, I think we will be less poverty-stricken next year."

"Gosh! How simply wonderful," exclaimed Marie.

"You really mean it? You're going to buy us a horse *and* a pony?" asked Jennet incredulously.

"Yes, truly. Now, for goodness' sake, go and help Tibbles get the tea. I'm ravenous."

"Oh dear, I ought to type," moaned Sheila.

"If I hear you wailing about that shocking novel again, I shall enter a lunatic asylum or become a monk," declared Patrick Pennyfield, splashing on paint.

"But I *must* finish it."

"All right, pack it up after tea and address the parcel to *The Kingham Typing Burea* and send it off first thing tomorrow. The cost will be about five pounds and you say you're charging four, so you will be a pound out of pocket and I'll gladly pay that if it'll stop you moping and whining."

"Oh, thank you, thank you very much," said Sheila.

"You'll have to send a letter with it, of course."

"Yes, of course," said Sheila.

"Daddy, if you buy us a horse and pony does that mean we won't go to Paris?" asked Charles.

"No, I'm taking you abroad whatever happens," said Patrick Pennyfield, "and if Lucien passes the school certificate I'll buy him a double-barrelled shotgun."

ARMADA BOOKS